Serenity
Bardic Eddas of Ry'gel

Lord Michael Ravenheart

Cadmus Publishing
www.cadmuspublishing.com

Published by Cadmus Publishing
www.cadmuspublishing.com
Port Angeles, WA

ISBN: 978-1-63751-385-9
Library of Congress Control Number:

To my children: You should have been the first to hear these tales. Better late than never they say.

Author's Note

Serenity,

Welcome to the world of Michael Ravenheart. Contained within the pages of this Fanbook is a compilation of works such as poems, legends, excerpts from my novels, a Dwarven Drinking song, and more. These glimpses were inspired by my homeworld of Proxima, which exists within the Alpha Centauri System in what is known as the 'Goldilock zone.'

But please indulge me and allow me to begin where I should have. Let us start with a few simple questions, and when you are done with this book, and after you have graduated and finished some of my other works, perhaps the true answer will come to you. So for now, allow me to pose them to you, and please reserve your answer until that future time.

What if the worlds that you have read about, the myths that have defined our existence and have taught us many of the life lessons that have made us who we are, were actually real? What if the writers of these tales, and these myths had actually traveled to these worlds, these times and seen them for themselves? And even better to contemplate, what if these writers had actually met some of the characters who populated their stories? And finally, what if these writers had actually come from the places they wrote about? Would that not be something?

When sitting down to write this book, I had to fight the urge to fill it and to create a work so exhaustive it would have become a tome that you could scarce carry, let alone read the whole of it in your lifetimes. Because, the memories from my homeworld, and the stories that I know from it, as well as the Histories that I have brought with me are almost neverending! Everyday, little supernovas are firing inside of my head to create new material, new Universes that are ever-expanding.

What I have included here is but a taste, a drop in an almost bottomless bucket of what exists within my mind. These stories are very personal to me and I hope that you enjoy them as much as I have writing them. And when it is all said and done and there comes the question of whether Proxima and Her people are real, I am confident that your answer will be a resounding…. YES!!!

Thank you for the time you have given me, and the chance you are giving to my world. May you never hunger, and may you never thirst.

Sincerely,

Lord Michael Ravenheart

ACKNOWLEDGMENTS

There are many people who have aided me in bringing my world to you dear reader, and it is they as much, if not more than me that you should thank. And so I shall do that for you. I could not have done this alone and without the constant encouragement of a few key people, I may not have gotten this far. First and foremost I would like to thank one of my very best friends, Robert "Kangi" Manship, who has not only been my Aide de Campe, but also my critic, my editor, and in some ways my co-developer of the world of Proxima and its characters. I owe him more than I will ever be able to re-pay and I feel that any-one who reads my works and appreciates it should tip their hats and lift a mug of ale or mead to my friend, the dwarf I call Kangi.

Others, whose names appear in the pages of many of my books and stories helped in their own small ways by providing me the space and the freedom that I need to work and to explore my world, to travel its breadth and to bring back its stories. They know who they are: the Hartshorns, Croteaus, the Breaults, the Darwazehs, the Kelemanns, the Lemues, the Doobies, the Mountains, the Perraults, the Sancyrs, the Rexs, Antonelli, the Juno, the Morynns, the Bearwicks, the Bartons, as well as the Aubuts and the Raymonds and others and they can find their tributes whenever they look within the pages of my stories and travel themselves to my world of Proxima.

To all of my beta readers: Travis 'Perseous' Bunnell, Jason 'Athemeus' Faucher, Barrett 'Siderogos' Hodgedon, and William 'the Ogre' Cote. Thank you for your help, comments and interests in proofreading my work.

To my friend, Justin Desrosiers, who has acted as my Tech Assistant, among other tasks and who will no doubt be fast on my heels with his own books. Thank you my friend for all of your help, and as I told you before, "If Michael Ravenheart wins, you win!"

And of course to my Literary Consultant and Temporary Agent, Miss A.J Dudley. Thank you for the belief you have had in me, and hopefully soon we will see our 'Seven Sisters' on Netflix or HBO. And a thank you to my friend Dan and his wife for typing my first novella, Book1: Doomslayer in the Road of the Seven Sisters series. To my typist, Miss Erica JO Cartrett, who is also working on her own books.

To all of my children whom I love, for above all else it is the legacy that I wish to leave them that motivates me the most.

Also to the mother of my children, Dianne, who served to inspire many of the characters in my larger novels. She is and shall remain a true love of my life, together or apart.

And last to all of you, the readers and hopefully… the Fans. Proxima is real. And through my novels and other future projects, I will be sure that this is the experience you will get from them. Someday, I will have built my Kingdom in Greece, modeled after my homeworld on Proxima, and it will be my further hope that some of you might join me there so that we could build for ourselves our own better life, living the way that the Elves of Proxima do…Without the dragons…. Hmm, BUT you never know! Until then please enjoy this book and keep your eyes out for my future works which will begin to arrive rapidly when finally my dream publisher picks me up! May you never hunger, may you never Thirst (Viata bestolden niennen, Lufala bestolden niennen.)

'Sabine struggled in her own way and mostly unseen by any of us. But there were moments when we would see that struggle most acutely. Especially when we were idle- when there was no external battle for her to sate her need. This was when her inner struggle would take hold. If she didn't isolate, if she was forced into a socializing role, she became irritable, prone to bursts of anger and fidgety. Often, she would forget things; times, places, where she was… But none of this affected her ability to be a great leader, or to keep us safe, though, I am not sure that she was of the same opinion on the matter…'

- From the Journey Book of Marlaya Morrowind

TABLE OF CONTENTS

THE ROAD OF THE SEVEN SISTERS
INTRO

(*'Together they faced a thousand and one foes...'*)

The seven auburn-haired women stood firm, poised before the Temple dedicated to the Goddess Athena, readying for the battle brewing. Their leader, the fiercest of them, bore no indication of fear or anger. There was no emotion at all. Only indifference showed as she scanned the enemy numbers across the dammed-up river. The enemy had stopped the Ravenwing a few miles upriver to make it passable for their troops. No small feat, since the riverbed was a good half mile or more across.

Born from Amazon fire, the leader, Sabine Valkyrie stood tall and menacing, her face however showing calm resolve while her one good eye focused and assessed their overwhelming situation.

The enemy stared back, taunting, testing and yelling obscenities at these seven 'sisters.' Like Sabine, the enemy knew that they had the women out numbered. Still the leader of the Night-shade Division of the King's army said nothing, *did* nothing, *revealed* nothing as she silently counted the odds that she and her 'sisters' faced.

From her right, one of the 'sisters', Kiera Ophiuccus smirked and said, "What say you Sabine? Should we fight? Or should we try and negotiate?"

The right corner of Sabine's mouth turned upward in an almost imperceptible grin as she responded, "What is it *you* would say, Kiera?" She asked.

Kiera smiled wide and after looking at the other sisters and receiving their nods of approval, she replied, "I say that it is as good a day as any to die."

Nodding in response, Sabine said, "So be it. Then chance for our friends across that river to have mercy is passed…" Raising her great sword high she glanced from left to right, and seeing the ferocity in each of her sisters' eyes, she whispered to them first… "If we die today sisters, join me for a toast to the Gods as stars in the sky, yeah?" The women nodded to their leader.

Her voice raising high and ringing out for all to hear and echoing across the divide she screamed, "Until we die!"

Together all of them gave answer… "WE FIGHT! FOR THE GODS!!!"

Laertes Royal Flag

"Your death is unwanted, for then you are useless.
It is your lives that we demand,
for only then can we ensure victory!"

Queen A'lonna
Speech to her DragonKnights

THE TIME OF THE OATH

Prophecy by: Apollonius Sicarius

Noble-born girl cloaked in lower-born guise
The Dragon veil cloaks the power in her eyes
During a time when the squire's ship sails
The Time of the Oath, Darkness unveiled

Quest for the Blade of the Angels remade
Royal house falters its power to fade
Many will pledge, even more to betray
Armies will march, 'tis the end of Old Ways

Blood shall reign from skies filled with fire
The Raven confessor will rest on funeral pyre
Promises made will breed oaths that are broken
A broken line fulfills Oaths left unspoken

A lost child royal baptised in dragon's blood
Will bring forth the dawn and ride the flood
Sorcerer's betrayal long ago sets the stage
The Time of the Oath brings about the New Age

A King like a pawn will hide truth from the light
But only his betrayal can put a kingdom aright.
A lost line restored from a commoner to make
Her death is ordained while lives are at stake

Her life will be brief but in death she prevails
To unite one and all, Heroe's soul can not fail
From Mortality's Cycle return they must
So hold dear their Love and Truth that you trust

Hope comes in waves and brings forth the light
A beacon of courage calling heroes to fight
Heroes upon the Dawn will appear
dispelling all doubt and banishing fear

Tomorrow's Children the Oaths are to make
Future of Elves and Proxima at stake
Proving their worth through valiant might
Remember the Virtues and keep them in sight

Demon's Bane, your foes they shall flee
Astride a great dragon though father he be
Wielding Revenge for your squire's last breath
make right by her life and give meaning her death

Forget not the hero whose cavernous forge
exists in the future through mists 'bove the gorge
Embraced in his dreams by dead lover at night
Through days in forge fires he keeps her in sight

Before the wars end, in blood they shall steep
A venomous Lord who will come from the Deep
Carrying the Darkness in chest born of Night
The Jackal-god comes, watch out for his bite

Light and Dark, Two Goddesses will fight
Both Full of vengeance and both Full of might
Only alliance can reconcile their pain
Proxima's end and Ancient Blood to Reign

Eclipse will announce Proxima's new start
Fire and Ice will at last share Their Hearts
Forged anew, She will end all the wars
For good or for ill Elves will worry no more.

Blade of all might, a legend Divine
First comes the voyage, One-handed squire to find
Carrying the Oath upon his sword-arm
She will ensure the squire comes to no harm

Over the oceans adventures in lost lands
Dark Titans fate lies in young squire's hand
The Blade is the curse, Set's Death is assured
Armies of Demons to the Deep will be lured

Bloodmetal keep in his caverns be born
New King of the Clans carrying Maghr'du's horn
Resting in peace before battles are won
Last Mountainborn King has raised his last son

With Moonblades and Bows, Books, and Bane
In the end Fates say: True-Blood will Reign
Medallion and Sceptre, Crown and Sword
Symbols of Freedom to fight off the horde

So be vigilant and warned and awake in that Time
Look for the Blade, Heroes of the Dawn are the signs
For the girl of the Bow who will announce it is here
Bringing us Hope, Light to Pierce Darkness and Fear

HOUSE LAERTES

**"Love, honour, compassion & bravery
The highest gift from the Gods"**

Liegehold: The entire island of New Avalon

Capitol: Sunstar

Hair Colour: Blond   **Eye Colour:** Indigo

Dragon Claws: (Clans): Rigel (amethyst) and Belial (yellow)

Patron God/ess: Zeus & Hera

Palladium: Zeus wearing togae, standing with a thunderbolt raised like a spear.

Primary Occupation: Government / Administration / Diplomacy / Advocacy

Bannerhouses: Aegina, Lakon, Icaria, Palinor, Avalonia, Morgan, Nicos, Rutile, Sabine, Shieldhal, Teraclea, Kythera, Valos, Morrighan, Xeno, Nephaline, Algar, Karpe, Cygnia, Virtus, Olympia Carridwen, Durothil, Hera, Aeris (of Thesos), Hermes, Kypress, Soma (Somdale), Faucher (of Shield), Thermopylus, Caratra, Croteau, Kelemann, Carpathos, Cygnia, Epirus, Lemnos, Nemea, Salonika, Milamar, Archeron, Olomar, Starr (of Ry'star), Rhea, Anuska, Pylos, Naxos, Brutus, Andros, Ionia, Kesan, Parga, Kavala, Rexus, Malisandre, Aubut, Rex

What is it? This life that you have led;
If you have been led, all of your life.

-Michael Ravenheart-

Darius' Plea

My love will you still love me when the war is over?
Or will the king take your love, your light and shut it from me.
Or maybe I shall die in this war, dreaming of your touch at night
the ghost of a tingle in my fingertips lingering unto Hades

My love perhaps it's over and I know not the truth of it
Or maybe you're here in my heart and that is enough to keep going
Or maybe when all is done the smoke of ill things will clear away
While the spirit of Hades is replaced by the touch I have longed.

My love, our times together in secret, are they enough for you.
Or do you long for that which we never wish to live without
Or it could be that the longing kills us before the war ever could.
But my spirit calls out to you in the darkest night with no return,

My love, your father demands a sacrifice for the death of his son.
Or maybe he would sacrifice you, his daughter in his hate for me.
Or perhaps he thinks I am incapable of rescuing you from our enemy
But love has a way to withstand the strongest devises to keep it.

Maretta, will I lose you now that the war is over?
Or are we finally free to become who we wish to be
Or is there a life waiting beyond the veil and the mist
For what exists beyond the door, only the Fey can know

My love, this is really our last chance to escape it all.
Or it is our sure-way into the blazing heat of death's inferno
Or maybe the judgment of the Gods for two forbidden Souls
Because we were never meant to be together, nor survive the war

My love, is this love worth living for?

King Keegan & his son Prince Kalhendor

WITHIN THE MISTS OF AVALON

AN ELVEN LEGEND

-Unknown Author- as recorded by Michael Ravenheart

Descended from stag, from wolf and bear
running through trees with their unbound hair.
Born to ascend through hunt and thru chase,
Came a proud people of noble Race
    Within the mists of Avalon
    The Lady blesses with sacred songs
    With nightingale or a mother's voice
    Teaches Her children of Freedom's choice.

In rituals to the moons they dance
naked, free, with bow and with lance.
Round the fires, nine times more,
Sing tales of Great Ayerlore
    Within the mists of Avalon
    On Ayerlore, old ways live on.
    Priestesses chant under full moons
    Asking Goddess for sacred boons

The Tribe comes first, and then the Clan
bringing life to woman and to man
The family benefits from these too
Then finally safety comes to you.
    Within the mists of Avalon
    Elves beware, of lands beyond
    where mighty beasts and gods conspire
    To add you to Their funeral pyre

Thirty-Three clans were said to depart,
wielding no maps, nor heavenly charts
fashioning ships from trees of Aegyptulup
They sailed away with a Goddess's Hope.
    Far beyond the mists of Avalon
    Our memories of home always to live on
    of ancient forests and plentiful times
    The families and Clans, Tribes left behind.

To foreign lands, too soon embraced
barren, hostile, a land without grace.
Tribes, clans and families were ripped apart
with them the lore, the tales of ethnic heart.
    Far beyond the mists of Avalon
    Pebbles cast into a great pond
    We wandered, were captured, then enslaved
    Living with nothing, without virtue, depraved.

Pray to the Goddess, She hears your call
She came with the Dwarves to rescue us all
Delivered to Morgos, we again rule ourselves
no longer held captive and calling us elves.
    Remember the mists of Avalon
    rebuilding ourselves, old ways live on
    Though changed, we remember old fires
    And Hope, wish and dream, and someday conspire,
    To return again through the mists of Avalon.

Thanatos and Myrflor 'Dragonbow' Woodvalley

DRAGONBOW: ORIGINS

In the aftermath of the fall and evacuation of the Amazonian homeland of Themis-kyra in the year 5E 2559, many of Her people sought revenge as a form of balm to their souls. There was a boom to the production of magickal weapons. During the Usurperwar's beginnings, as the war with the Ultors would later be called, weapons of power were reserved, or created for officers in the military, knights of noble birth, and the lords and ladies of a House or banner. But after the fall of the Kingdom of the great House of Valkyrie, a demand was made by Queen Tumarra, Lady of the House, for all warriors from her lands, noble-born Aldari or low-born Alnari to be able to have crafted a magickal weapon of their choosing.

The Crown would not argue the Lady Valkyrie, and issued a Royal summons for all those who knew of the arcane magickal arts to team with weapon and armour smiths throughout the freelands, even employing the Dwarven Dragonsmiths who were the exclusive crafters of the most powerful bloodmetal weapons in the known world.

Over the years, many of those weapons and armour, as well as much of those arcane arts, have been lost. There can still be found a few very rare items left from that time. One such weapon is the famed Dragonbow. It has been preserved for thousands of years since its first owner wielded it in battle against the forces of the Blood Queen, Meghan Ultor. It was believed to have been made by the gods themselves.

This bow was made for Clarissa Valkyrie, niece of the Lady Tumarra herself. It was made of a silver leg bone from an immensely large Eldarr Dragon named Fireclaw the Red who gave his life in defense of the Queendom of Themis-kyra before its fall. The bones were smuggled out with Queen Tumarra and the others who fled. The bone was then given into the hands of one of the best bowyers in the land, an Alnari man named Rikker Woodvalley, and together with a dwarven Dragonsmith, and the best enchanters, they devised a bow so powerful that it was believed fit only for Artemis Herself.

Paired with four magickal bloodmetal rings, it was given not to the Moons Goddess, but to Queen Tumarra's own niece, who served as a Dragonknight in the queen's own daughter's elite squad called 'The Nightshade Division.' The Dragonbow would prove to be one of the most powerful weapons ever devised by Elves and Dwarves. After the deaths of the famed 'Seven Sisters,' of which Clarissa Valkyrie was among that number, the bow was rescued from the battlefield and would eventually make it to Warmaiden Hall when at last Themis-kyra was liberated from the Usurpers years later. The rings that once powered the famous bow were never recovered, but it is said that it is nonetheless, a formidable and magickally powerful weapon. Of course, until one comes who proves to be worthy of it, we continue to wonder whether this is so.

Excerpt: Time of the Oath Chronicles
Book Two: Dragonbow Legacy

"Aspirations"

"Please. . Oh Please Alleron," Pleaded the young girl. The old bard could only smile at the "green hair's" enthusiasm. Like all of the children, they look forward to the tale spun by Alleron, the most famous bard in the lands of Ry'gel.

"Tell us another tale of the Seven Sisters. . ." She continued to beg, and was quickly joined by the rest of the children, until the bard could refuse no more. Smiling, he looked down at all of them, and finally his eyes settled on the young girl who had begun this mutiny of his time.

"Surely Myrflor," He said to her, "I have told you enough tales to fill that old tavern over there. If you'd have written them all down we could turn the tavern into a library."

"Still," She complained, "You have been here but a mid-sec, and told no tales. And already you were preparing to leave."

Alleron chuckled. "Bards do have other jobs beyond the telling of tales, young one. We are also messengers. And right now, I have an urgent message for someone who is extremely important. . ."

This news only served to excite the young girl even more, and she immediately pried him for more. "Who is the message for?" She asked. "What does it say?"

Alleron rubbed his smooth chin as he thought it over. His eyes squinted at the young girl, and a mischievous smile came upon his face. "I suppose that I could tell you. But if I do . . . you will let me go in peace?"

The young girl thought it over a moment. What if the message was not that important, or whom it was for was not so exciting? Then they will have traded an exciting story for some boring old news. It was a dilemma, and Myrflor, as the children's self-appointed leader, would need to decide.

"Never mind." She said finally. "I think that we all would rather hear a story."

With a glint in his old Aldari eyes, Alleron smiled and nodded. "Very well . . . Then where was I?"

"The last time you were here," began one of the other children, a white haired boy named Castius Altair. "You were telling us about the Seven Sisters thwarting the Blood Queen at Edge Rock, and how they had ruined her plans to take the Edge Rock River."

The bard held up a finger as if suddenly remembering. "Oh yes, that is right. Edge Rock."

The young girl looked over at Castius with an approving nod, and both sat down next to one another, and were soon followed by the others in the group. At first the old Elven man just stared into the eyes of his eager audience, and soon even some of the adults from Avonsdale were gathered to hear another tale told by the infamous bard. Finally he's settled on the young Elven girl Myrflor. For her, it was, that he was really here. For her he would tell her all that he knew of the Seven Sisters, and more. And he certainly knew their tale most intimately. For her, if she had asked, he would tell her all that was needed to ensure that she fulfilled her destiny.

Myrflor Woodvalley, who was born in the nearby hamlet of Faerieglenn, was a bit of an oddity to the other children, with her green low-born elven hair and the unique silver stripe that ran down one lock of it on her right side. No children had ever been born like her, and there were those children who could make a point of it and tease her. But Myrflor never let it bother her. Instead she had more than once proven herself to these young elves, and to many of the adults as well.

Her parents had told her that the silver stripe in her hair was due to the rare sickness that had almost cost her her life when she was an infant. But the bard knew better, and it was for this reason that he chose this city to tell his stories, returning every couple months to look in on the young girl who could count even the Archmagus Leontes Juno as an uncle, even though he was Aldari, and she only a low-born Alnari Elf.

"Sabine Valkyrie was not one to go long without a fight," the bard began. "After Edge Rock, the Nightshade Division had little to do. But Sabine would soon receive word that the Blood Queen was moving troops to the lands of Annwin. And for the great leader this could not happen. . . She moved her own troops to stop the Blood Queen at Caledahn."

The story went on for some time and the children, as always were hooked. They would hang on every word, listening with rapt attention. None more so than Myrflor Woodvalley. In her there was a hero, like those of old. And little did the young girl know, she would soon not only be a great hero, but she would join roads with one of the most prolific heroes in history.

Eventually the story, or this addition of it, came to an end, and when the bard announced this there was a collective "aww!" from the crowd, including no too few of the adults. But for the first time, Myrflor was not in that number. Instead she stood slowly, smiling and satisfied from the story. The bard looked at her with a quizzical eye, a small, interested smile upon his face as his assistant, the bardic apprentice Perseous Rex came sauntering over carrying their bags. "The horses are ready Alleron." He said to his teacher. "We really should be going."

"Yes, yes Perseous." The bard said with some annoyance as the young girl and her lira Kelli came up to him. "In a moment." He responded, shooing the apprentice away. "Serenity mistress of Faerieglenn," Alleron said to Kelli in greeting.

"Serenity to you Bard Alleron." Kelli replied. "I want to thank you for your tales. Myrflor does love them, and we very much appreciate that you take the time for the children."

"It is my pleasure of course." Said the bard. "After all," he looked down at the young girl, "it is they who will be the heroes of their own story someday. And who knows, I may yet be telling the tales of Myrflor Woodvalley before too long."

Myrflor blushed a deep crimson and gave the widest smile he had ever seen her display.

Looking down at her daughter, Kelli said, "Go say goodbye to your friends Myrflor."

Myrflor nodded and smiled again at Alleron. "Thank you again Ser Alleron." She said to him.

"You are especially welcome Myrflor," he told her before the girl ran off to join her friends. Looking back to Kelli he said, "She is a very special girl."

"Mmhm. She is." Said the girl's mother. "After her sickness was cured by Archmagus Juno, I still watched over her, every night, waiting for the illness to come back. I had been so resigned to losing her that the possibility still remained in my mind. But now, seeing her so . . . she is so alive and strong. The only thing left to remind of that time is that odd silver stripe in her hair. . ."

"Yes." The bard mused. "A result of the healing that the Archmagus had performed. Tell me, does he still come 'round to visit her?"

Kelli nodded. "Every year on her Nosta. He rarely ever misses a visit. If not he, then his bond-mate Alika comes."

Guessing that there was more to Kelli's sending Myrflor off, the bard asked, "Is there something that I can do for you Mistress?"

When Kelli looked back at him there was a tear running down her cheek. Dashing it away she said, "All that she ever talks about are the Seven Sisters from your legends, and some of the other heroes. She dreams of being one of them, and it makes her happy when you reinforce that possibility in her. I appreciate that, even if her father does not. He is a good man, do not get me wrong." Kelli reassured the bard. "But if he had it his way, she would become a bowyer like he and never go on any adventures. And this is simply not my girl. She is destined to become a hero, as you have said before."

"Mmm, she is." the bard confirmed as he pulled the pipe from his bag and began filling it with Kannibi leaf.

Kelli looked at the bard curiously. "How is it that you know?" She asked him. "I mean to say that I am her mother, her lira. It is my job to know the dreams of my daughter, and her potential. But you ser?"

"There is much that I see in the fabric of another's life mistress." He replied. "I know a hero when I see one." He chuckled "I have seen enough of them in my lifetime, and told the tales of more than that."

Finally Kelli said, with a bit of sadness edging her voice, "Still, thank you for that. For your stories. I only wish that I could be around to see her. . ." Another tear ran down her cheek, and she just let it go. Shaking her head she said thank you again and bid the bard farewell. Alleron watched her go, curiosity etched on his face when Perseous came back with the horses.

"Ready?" Said the apprentice. Alleron watched the woman gather her daughter and head toward the western bridge out of town. "Yes." He said finally looking back at Perseous. "Yes. Let us go."

"Do you think it wise?" Asked Perseous as they headed through the South gate of the city of Avonsdale. The sun shone down brightly, and the weather had become warmer, perfect for the coming festival season in this colder part of the country.

"Do I think 'what' wise?" the bard asked him.

"You reveal too much to the child." The apprentice responded. "Perhaps before she is ready."

"You speak to me of wisdom, servant of Zeus. . ." The bard scoffed. "ME!" Suddenly the bard's clothing melted away to be replaced by that of gleaming silver armor. His male features were transformed into that of a beautifully radiant grey-eyed woman. She had a spear in her hand to replace the staff she had carried and she wore a long sword on her hip. If her Chrysaor noticed the change he made no indication and only nickered, his ears twitching to remove a fly that had tried to land.

Unphased, the apprentice began to change form as well, becoming a stunning young woman with long flowing Violet hair that changed colours in the sunlight, like an oil slick. And although the grey-eyed one had her own wings, hers did not show. But the apprentice's shoulders erupted with a fan of feathers the color of a rainbow.

"What does it matter?" The grey-eyed one asked.

"I suppose that it does not . . ." the other said in a huff. "Still, why do you do it? Why do we keep coming here? If you are going to tell the child of her future, then do it and let us get on with more important matters. The longer that you dally, and put it off, the more chance that Zeus will find out."

"This is why I have you Iris." The Grey-eyed one said. "Without His Messenger, who is there to tell the All-father what I am about?" She gave Iris, the Apprentice and Messenger Goddess a pretty smile.

"Then tell me oh wise Athena." Iris responded in annoyance. "Why do you do it? What is this truly about?"

"There are some things that have not been told to you lesser gods, that have been revealed to us. I do this for one, as a favour. But most of all I do it because if I were to tell the girl that she will inspire the greatest heroes of the next generation, that she herself were more than this mortal life, and that she will someday save the planet, it could fill her with such fear that could hinder her ability to become just that. She would become uncertain and she might falter at the most crucial moment and fail in her true destiny. How could a mortal mind even be prepared for such news that they are the saviour of their race, and the Races of the Gods?

"But. . ." The Goddess continued. "Tell her the story of a real champion, one that has already done such things. . . Now they have someone to aspire to become. Myrflor will spend these young years of influence admiring and emulating the bravery of Sabine Valkyrie and her 'Seven Sisters,' of Marlena Valinor and her defeat of the Blood Queen. She will tell her friends of the glorious adventures of these heroes. She will think of all of the amazing things that they did, and she will say to herself, "I can do all of those things too, if I work really hard!"

Athena took a long pause as they continued on horseback, their chrysaors trotting along and rising into the air on some invisible road that ascended into the heavens.

"Would you lay Mount Olympos onto the back of that child, tell her to carry it a distance, and expect that she could hold it steady?" Athena asked Iris finally. "Or would you tell her of the honor and the glory that awaited her when she enters the Palace of the gods at the top of the Mount, and give her the reason to climb it?"

Athena looked over at the Messenger of Zeus, not really expecting an answer before continuing. "Over the next few years, Myrflor will grow stronger out of admiration for the 'Seven Sisters' and for the hero Marlena Valinor and her dragonsteed Evenride. She will become a champion herself because of them and she will inspire one of the greatest heroes this world would ever know. And when that day comes. . . when she sees for herself the Veil and hears the Call of the Mistress of Death upon the fateful winds of Imminent Doom- she will know what these stories were about. And at that moment, on her Road into Hades, she will be able to become the Goddess that she was born to be. . ."

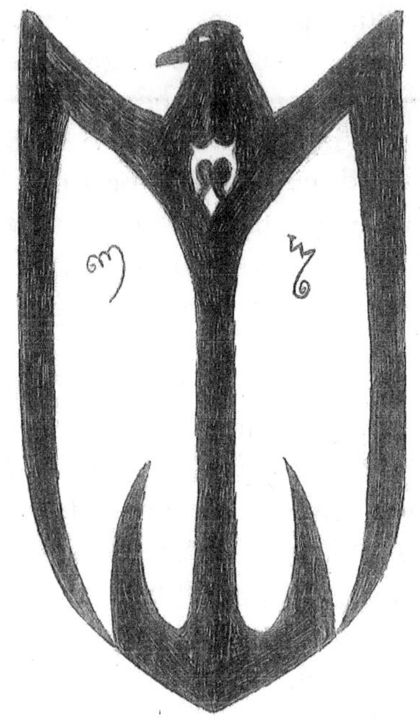

HOUSE RAVENCREST

"Justice and True of Purpose"

Liegehold: From North meeting lands of House Keto to the south at lands of Houses Arachne and Silvermane. From West at the Necklace Canal to the Eastern-most Coastline.

Capitol: Ravencrown

Haircolour: Black   **Eye Colour:** Purple

Patron God/ess: Athena, Artemis & Apollo

<u>Palladium:</u> Athena wearing a war-kilt & breastplate with a dragon-head upon it. In one hand she holds a sword above her head in a horizontal, defensive posture. In her left hand she holds (weight) scales. Her hair is bundled behind her head. At her side is a open-faced helm with a thick horse-hair comb.

<u>Primary Occupation:</u> Constablatory / Judiciary / Litigation / Governance

<u>Bannerhouses:</u> Draco, Elmfast, Caledahn, Miren, Riverworn, Maidenwell, Calburn, Druidan, Xandria, Lud, Elmfast, Delphinus, Smallfort, Sancyr, Anatase, Altaunt, Marius, Ravencry, Lordis, Cervantes, Draco, Trona, Ara, Hydrus, Auriga, Nightstar, Verator, Crixus (of Deepwood) Merewynn, Aldaris (of Axel), Aldaran, Siefort, Diwaza, Gurard, Morynn, Athana, Hurne, Faerieglenn, Kuhn, Loholt, Vicar, Bedwyr, Bedwin, Coharie, Dhisana, Sebille, Sarlinna, Ravenscroft (bastards), Auriga, Doobie, Steady, Rexus, Raymond

Lady-Knight A'lonna Ravencrest

THE TIME OF THE OATH CHRONICLES
BOOK ONE: RAVENCREST LEGACY

PROLOGUE

On a moonlit night, thousands of years ago . . .

Fog crept through the lowland clearing, moving in tendrils of mist, thick like a blanket across the ground and rising ever so slightly when it hit an obstruction, only to crawl its way over the obstacle and continue on. The sounds of the forest creatures were a distance away but served as a low hum that added to the ritualistic atmosphere like background music, as the robed figures chanted in unison the words of prophecy that would call forth the Pneumos needed to make the ceremony a success.

Only two amongst these black-robed figures did not join the others. One, who wore the white robe of the Elder mages, simply gripped his staff with silent worry that something would go terribly wrong. He was risking his life, and the lives of every mage in this gathering on a ritual that had thus far ended in failure. Each attempt prior had ended in the gruesome death of the infant newborn being subjected to the magickal process.

But this time was different. Prior to this attempt, the white robed figure had not been present to oversee his own apprentice's terrible experiments using first, human children, and more recently Elven children. Humans were one thing, a low caste creature, made with what was left over when the Gods had made the Elves and all of the other superior creatures. But using an Elven child, and worse, killing it, should have not only had the White Robe's student expelled from their Order, it should have resulted in his death.

But this student was different from the rest. uncaring and unapologetic in his experiments and administrations. Over the years the White Robe had learned that this student was possessed of a dark spirit. But what was he or any of his fellow mages to do? None would disobey the request, the veiled command of the king when His Majesty specifically asked that his nephew be allowed into the Temple of Aradia.

And now, on this night celebrating the annual Divine birthday of their Patron Goddess, the White Robe prayed that he had made the right choice in agreeing all of those years ago to teach the young Prince all that he knew. Their lives depended on whether they succeeded in this task this night. And although the White Robe stood by to lend his magickal assistance if it became necessary, if they were to fail in this, the King's nephew be damned, His Majesty would have all of their heads. And if not he, then her Highness, the Queen, . .

If it had not been for the collective visitation of the Goddess Herself, to all those who were present this night, none of them would be here. The White Robe would never have agreed to this, and would have found every possible way to stop this, what he viewed as madness. And still, even with the will spoken by the Goddess Herself, the White Robe still held reservations.

"This had better work Antares." He had said to his student before the ritual had begun. "Because if it does not . . . " The White Robe looked over at the thirteenth member, robed in red, a small bundle cradled in their arms, and he needed to say no more to the apprentice.

"I assure you Master," The young mage replied, "The Goddess is behind us in this. Nothing can go wrong. . . "

Lucius sighed at his apprentice's estimation. He knew that although the Goddess may be behind them, the Fates were fickle creatures who need not heed the wills even of the Gods and the Goddesses. "Yes my young student. . . it is hubris like that which causes the wrong to be precisely what happens."

Lucius Gryffyn had been the Archmagus of his Order for hundreds of years. He was the very mage, thousands of years before this night that had discovered the method to hatching the Eldarr Dragons. By accident of course, and at the cost of the life of his own mentor, Tommen Juno, who was then the Archmagus. Years later he would also discover that after a dragon was hatched, which took much magick and the sacrifice of an Elven heart, that another heart from someone who had willingly donated it, could be placed into the fresh dragon egg and then magically sealed again, to be stored for millennia if need be and used to hatch another dragon at a later time.

The Order of Aradia were scientists. They studied every aspect of magick, and when this method of hatching dragons was discovered, a special branch of mages had been opened to study the magick of dragons, and all of the ways that they could be hatched. When the method of the containment of the hearts was discovered, a small group of the mages got into their heads that live creatures might also be able to be stored inside the eggs. This resulted in many deaths, and those who were responsible were expelled, and their own leader was even executed by the King. So, when Lucius's own student, nephew of the King began doing the same thing, taking up where the former mages had left off, Lucius had immediately put a stop to it.

And now, here he was, at a time when he was sure he would be in the waning years of his tenure as Archmagus, ready to place an infant child into a dragon egg, possibly condemning the poor innocent to torment it needn't suffer, all because of some unknown reasoning handed down from a Goddess. Lucius had never had reason to doubt the Gods before. But then, the Gods and the Goddesses had been absent from the world for countless millennia. None had seen them in ages. Who was to say that the apparition that they all saw was the Goddess and not some trickster God who wanted them to condemn themselves by sacrificing one of the King's own children.

Softly the eleven other members chanted the words given them by the Goddess Aradia. their hands were still raised above their heads, while the shell of a purple Dragon's egg lay open on the altar. The fire blazed behind the altar, and the black-flamed candles flickered ever so gently even as the wind began to pick up around the circle.

Orosta Avolone ' en Dharasha,
Caitala Otani itan
Arayante Lu'uumenquentah 'ah
Caitala ek Malon Otani
Ataran yuleh hruvalye namarie
Caitala Avatea'

Overhead a storm had gathered. The two moons of Artemis, one on each side of the sky remained uncovered by the rapidly thickening black clouds. The dark sky flickered with lightning, and the world around them erupted with sound suddenly, as the flashes of red and purple lightning was followed by the booming of Zeus's thunder. There was no rain, nor a threat of rain as thick bolts of electricity raced across the sky. But whether the display was one of anger from the King of the Gods or one of joy, none but a weather augur would know.

As thunder shook the ground, wind howled around them and trees bowed with its power, but none, not even one candle flame inside of the magick circle were affected. Only the fire itself seemed to care as it suddenly roared to life, and the chanting from the mages grew louder and more urgent.

Lucius moved to the red-robed figure, who held the tiny bundle. . the figure, whose face remained shadowed in darkness, seemed reluctant to hand the little girl over when the White Robe reached for her. It was in this moment that Lucius truly felt fear and his own hesitation.

"Your Highness, it is time." Said Lucius. And for the first time, the head came up from staring down at the babe in his arms and the face of the king could be seen in the flickering firelight. He looked skeletal, worry lines under his eyes, with a hint of sadness and guilt. The queen did not know, she COULD NOT know or even the king would not be spared her wrath.

The king nodded and bent his head again to kiss the child on her tiny forehead. "I'm sorry Lorna, my beautiful daughter." He said to her before handing her off to the White Robe. He did not remain to see the ritual completed. He could not. He needed to get back to the queen, who even now slept, a magickally induced sleep. When she woke, she will have learned that she had lost her child, her golden daughter, Lorna.

✦ 31 ✦

RAVENCREST LEGACY

BOOK I IN THE TIME OF THE OATH CHRONICLES

"You have a very good friend in Rianna, you know." Rynn commented

"Do I?" A'lonna scoffed. "If she *were* so good, the bottle would have already been waiting for me when I woke."

Rynn Eversoar sighed in frustration. "Possibly *TOO* good for you." He said and went to pacing, not unlike her Ata when he was about to lecture her over something she had failed to do. "That girl is risking everything just being around you, you know." He went on and A'lonna rolled her eyes. "Her Dignitas, Her family, Her reputation. It is why she sent Myflor home to Avonsdale."

"I did not ask her to." A'lonna retorted, a little petulant for a Lady-Knight. "She could've chosen to leave me as well. What would it matter?

Rynn's heart could not help but to go out to his best friend's daughter. But he could not let sympathy get in the way of what needed saying. "You are right, she could have," he agreed. "And if I was her, I might have. But alas she did not. She chose the risk because that is what friends do... What *Family* does. She loves you. We *ALL* love you. And seing you like this..." His head dropped slightly. "I can tell you what your Ata would say... And you know as well as I what that is. He would be very disappointed in you. I am very disappointed in you."

A'lonna half-drunkenly swept his comment aside with a wave of her hand. "Still, you can join the line." A'lonna replied. "And as for my Ata.... He is dead, lest you forget, so.... His opinion hardly matters, now does it."

"Do not make light or jest of it you insolent little child!" Rynn spoke angrily. The rebuke brought A'lonna's head up and tears began forming in her bloodshot eyes.

"You will listen to me, or you will not." He continued. "But my own conscience is clear as I have done what I can to honor my old friend. I could not save him…" Rynn said, a soft sob choking his throat. "But have tried to save you. And now that I have said my piece, I will be on my own way and you will hear me no more."

"Thank the Gods!" Exclaimed A'lonna. Then pointing toward the table next to him she said, "But before you go, can you pass me that bottle?"

THE LADY OF PALE WOOD

By Michael Ravenheart

The lady of Pale wood floated 'tween the tall trees
None to pay heed to her sorrow and pain
No lords nor their ladies to lay claim to her soul
to the life the lords had left stained
So moving and moaning she glides through the mists
a victim of their privilege and pride
Like a mare they could beat and rut time and again
on whom the lords and ladies could ride
 And never once she complained
 Samara never complained

Within her womb a foal they had whelped
her disgrace the order of the day
Until down a well in the middle of Pale Wood
Samara went, and that is where she shall stay
Low-born she was and so no one would care
a servant too low to feel shame
There were none to wonder where poor Samara had gone
only commenting… "The mare had gone lame."
 Samara never complained
 How could the ghost complain

Hours she lay broken, afraid and alone
only One to hear her pleas
Death there to offer the peace long desired
but her soul would never go free
Now she rages, cries, mourns and again
the son they had taken to fight
But Samara still looks for the son through the days
and she haunts the Pale wood at night

And ever will she cry
for the son that had died

If you go to Pale Wood, go with Heart in your hands
and be sure to listen to the Knight
Cry and wail and moan though she will
be sure that you stay within sight
She has waited and wandered, wanting someone to hear
of the son she had left to the Light
His bones she will covet, she will cherish and more
if just this one wrong could finally be put right
    Then she will never again complain
    Samara will finally be without pain

In our darkest moment, and through our foulest, most regrettable acts, from our deepest despair, sometimes comes the birth of our greatest redemption; our proudest and most noble deed. Indeed! For where else is there to go when you are already at the bottom?

- Michael Ravenheart-

"Beware the Wandering One – for he announces Doom!"

- the Oracle Kianna

FROM 'THE TIME OF THE OATH SAGA'

HYMN OF THE DRAGONSMITH

Boroleas Mts. - Dragonforge of Gordek Mountain born – 7E 2053

Visions assaulted A'lonna's mind, confusing and fragmented, things that she could not recognize. The cavern of the Dragonsmith and the great golden serpent forge had disappeared and it appeared to the Lady-Knight that she was being transported some-where else entirely. And from somewhere around her, combined with the echoing strikes of a hammer came a song, low and deep, sung as if by a thousand burly voices.

[A Dwarven hammer rises and falls
The heartbeat to the Dragonsmith's call
bloodmetal wrought from volcanic fount
Sacred duty we work 'neath sacred mount.]

A'lonna could feel the intense heat from the dragonforge coating her body, enveloping her father's armour. And yet, the heat was not unbearable as her mind drifted into other times and back again. She could see Raylor standing before her, his hammer and the molten bloodmetal being applied to the armour she wore while the forge fire of the golden dragon continued its slow and steady flame, coating them both, licking their skin and the blood-metal skin armour once belonging to her Ata, the great Mjendor Ravencrest. Beyond the flames she could see the blood-mage, his head turned upward to the open roof of the cavernous forge, his mouth emitting a blue light into the sky, while a red beam flowed from his right hand and toward she and Raylor creating the magickal shield that only allowed the fire to melt the metal, and not their skin with it.

And as the scene in front of her changed again and the cavern fell away, she heard yet more chanting. In this newest scene, over forty dwarves carried pieces of blood metal to a volcanic river nearby, dropping the metal beneath its hot surface while singing their song.

[Magick heard through voices of stone
Music from which ancient powers are known
From burning rock and by hardened tree
This bloodmetal forge Dwarven mystery]

[In the cavernous halls of Mountainborn
Lives the mighty forges at Hartshorn
Sacred Powers harnessed Void of Light
Hidden Lessons will be kept from Sight]

Dwarves moved one-by-one to the river of lava, singing the song, their faces merry and full of joy in what they were doing. On the other side of the molten river there sat a giant purple dragon, its head bobbing to the tune while the dwarves moved to separate anvils and began to fashion the tools or weapons appointed them, all the while continuing with their song. A'lonna felt her heart swelling with joy in their song, their hammers rising and then falling in time with the tune like metallic drums.

[Hestia to breathe life, the bellows hot air
Bloodsong is kept safely in Dwarven care
When the song rings right in Ancient fane
The magick will give to the smith Her name

In the cavernous halls of Mountainborn
Flows the blood of Olden Gods, and oaths are sworn
Although the metal bends to their will

The magick within can not stay still]

One by one, the dwarven smiths walked toward the molten river, their finished projects held before them and one-by-one, each jumped into the lava of bloodmetal. The magma swirled and churned as they sunk beneath, changing colors from red to yellow and then to violet, flowing out of the mountain forge and into a bright sunlit valley.

A'lonna followed the river out and put her arm up protectively as her violet eyes adjust to the sun's light. Without realizing how it'd happen, she was surrounded by others, a whole legion of elven warriors, all dressed in their finest bloodmetal armour. A'lonna herself no longer wore her father's armour, but instead a gold-trimmed double breasted purple jacket. At her side sat a sword all too familiar to her, the King's word Lightning. Inspecting herself further she realized that her hair was blond and she wasn't a woman any longer, but a man.

Across the molten river stood a dwarven king who moved toward her upon a magickal bridge that spanned the lava flow. As he came closer she could see that he held reverently before him a palm-sized medallion of reddish-gold bearing the Laertes House Crest upon it and encircled with many runes that were unrecognizable to her. This was the medallion of kingship and A'lonna was seeing through the eyes of a king. When his lips moved, the dwarf only told her that many had sacrificed their lives to see the oathbinding medallion restored. Of their own volition, A'lonna's hands came forward and took it from the dwarven king, lifting it then over her head and placing it around her neck.

[The door reveals the way like an open heartbeat
To give the metal name its magick becomes your part
Strike the hammer hard, ring it loud and true
Its way shall open to let its power through

Pour the grog into upturned hand at the gate
Stay firm as axe falls and seal your Fate

Pay the holy fee to enter the ancient gorge
And find the secret of Hephaestos' forge.]

A fire rose around A'lonna and all of the elves and dwarves nearby. The river itself ran as if over a waterfall, but instead of the edge disappearing, the lava ran upward and into the sky. The elves and dwarves were gone now and she wore her father's armour once again. The lava flowed upward and into the side of a massive mountain before her. Looking around revealed the familiar landscape in the crescent mountains near Mistgate.

The chanting continued as from a crevice before her, billowing black smoking issuing from its depths, the form of a dwarf appeared. His clothes and beard and hair was blackened and scorched and smoking. He was burnt and bleeding and gasping for breath. There was something familiar about him and when his eyes met hers there was a moment of recognition in them.

He coughed and said only one word before passing out at the edge of the crevice. "*Bloodryder.*" He called out.

A shadow passed overhead and answered the question in her mind as three dragons and their riders dropped from the sky and landed near the prone dwarf. A'lonna's heart thudded as she recognised them. It was her father Mjendor, on his black steed, Rakkinor, and his two best friends, Rynn and the former King Aron on their dragons, Freya the blue and Luciferus the silver.

Then all around her went black.

As light returned she was somewhere else and again surrounded by people she did not recognize. But like her cousin and best friend Rianna, they had the Valkyrie-Auburn hair.

Soldiers scoured a battlefield and the Aubun-haired women moved nearby, all killing enemies that remained alive. Below her, trapped beneath an eponodari was an orc. He was alive and although he looked like any orc she had ever seen, he was different. He wore bloodmetal armour, which was not unheard of to A'lonna, but he also bore the crest of the Silvermane on his pauldron. A'lonna held a sword out to him, one that she did not even recognize. It warbled with reddish glowing energy like liquid lava along its blade and upon the hilt beneath red crystals was the word *Krimzin*

"What have you got there Sabine?" Came a voice next to her. A'lonna didn't recognize the voice, nor the name that she was being called and when she looked up she saw a young woman, new to knighthood and for reasons unknown to her, A'lonna had an overwhelming need to cry, to sob and to rage all at once.

[In the Ancient caverns of Mountainborn
lies in wait the sacred Dwarven Horn
Calling forth protectors of beastly might
to once again take up the fight.

Remember those who give up their souls
to ensure the forges remain whole
And forget not the ones who'll announce the Doom
And the Time of the Oath that is coming soon.]

THE TIME OF THE OATH : THE TOWER

By Apollonius Sicarius

Behold! The Beacon of Holy Might
Shall answer in Times of Angels' Flight
A warning heard, the mother recite
The mountain cracks amidst the fight
All shall flee the mother's plight
The Tower, standing proud, shall vanish from sight.

Concept Cover, *Ravencrest Legacy*

HOUSE VALKYRIE

"Until I die, I fight!"

Liegehold: The Amazon lands encompass the entire Islands of Themis-Kyra

Capitol: Warmaiden Hall

Hair Colour: Auburn   **Eye Colour:** Violet

Dragonclaws: Fireclaw (red) and Cazna (blue)

Patron God/ess: Nike and the Olympians

Palladium: Unknown winged & Armoured Goddess, assumed to be Nike

Primary Occupation: Ambassadorial, Military, Horse Breeders/Ladies, Griffin-Riders, Pegasus Breeders

Bannerhouses: Drakanos (of Drakan), Morrowind (of Antiope), Everrun, Eretrea, Aris, Lisandra, Ophiuccus (of Ophiucci), Nicolo (of Nicolopolos), Isis (of Asai), Clairum (of Astabi), Ilsa, Nike, Falconeri, Darwazeh, Gurardis (Garuda), Inissa, Ostara, Essen, Talon, Alyssar, Mare, Rycroft, Martley, Mateer, Heron, Corr, Kell, Couser, Croftward (bastards), Antonelli

A BARD'S TALE

WORDS OF TALIESIN

The tavern was busy this night.

'A good crowd,' thought the Bard as he walked to the back of the room. This bard was well-known to this high-classed establishment. They recognized his 'Laertes-blond' hair. But more than this, although he came from a banner that served the royal Laertes family, he wore a pin-clasp that held this auburn cloak with its sigil for the amazon House Valinor, his mother's House. And although his mother came from Auburn-haired warrior House of Amazon's, he was no warrior. He left such tasks to his elder siblings while he was content to report their exploits through verse.

Many of these wealthy patrons had come to the diplomatic city of Sunstar for the senatorial and none would miss the opportunity to come to this tavern to hear the famed Bard, Taliesin Croteau, whose musical poetry and tales of valiant battle could make the hardiest warriors shed a tear. His tales were exciting and terrible adventures populated by characters so prolific none who heard them could forget their names in their lifetimes.

The bard knew the tavern-owner who was friends with his Lira before her untimely death years before. At dinner with the tavern master and his family only last week, Taliesin had tried a new tale on them and they had been moved, begging him to tell it in the tavern. This tale, however, touched a very personal and emotional chord inside of him and he'd almost not written it at all, it'd be so difficult.

Sitting upon the stool at the back of the tavern-room he proceeded to pluck at the strings of his lyre with his lucky dragon bone plectrum in order to tune it- a procedure that'd become more of a tradition than an actual need. Meanwhile the entire tavern, seeing that he was about to begin, grew quiet knowing that whatever the tale tonight, it would leave them moved.

The scent of ois'gee, coffee, food and smoke mingled in the air- a combination of smell he'd grown to love over the years. The tavern master brought over a mead just as he was finishing the ministrations to his strings. He paused in the plucking to drink down and savor the familiar Valkyrie mead, the mead of his Lira's people.

Finally the plectrum, guided by his hand, began to pluck the strings softly on some notes, and roughly on others a sad song of longing. Each of the patrons who come to hear it settled in for what was no doubt was going to be one of the most epic poems of the bard's career.

'I am no warrior, this is true.' He began while the song went on. 'I leave such ambition to my elder brothers and sisters. They take after our Lira you see, whom you all know as Duchess Marle-na Valinor, the hero who rid us of the Blood Queen.'

The song continued, turning even sadder.

'It is from her that I received the story for my lyric,' he told the audience and still the song became impossibly more sad and lonely.

'It was when I was very small and my siblings had been fighting with each other. She had called us all together and she told me this story- a tale of Seven Sisters who traveled a warrior's road togeth-er. These sisters were bonded not by blood, but by the forges of battle. Against all odds, these seven women held back the tide of one thousand enemy troops to protect a sacred artifact until reinforcements could arrive. I am sure that you have all heard this story before. But I assure you that you have never been told it like this, in words given to me by someone who was there to witness the heroics of these Seven Sisters. Someone who traveled the road with them for a time, until their momentous and valiant end.'

Without another word, as the music began its own sonorous lament, he began to tell them about the road of the seven sisters.

THE ROAD OF THE SEVEN SISTERS

By Michael Ravenheart

Prologue

Adventure is naught if one has no tales,
Men and women whose adventures prevail
Elves you see, by nature are heroes, it's true.
Lord and Lady Knights there are ne'er too few.
So hear ye these words of heroines so bold.
Whose lives, though brief, future heroes to mold.
They lived in a time while Ry'gel was at war.
Seven Lady-Knights live to this day through our lore.
When a person is measured by noble act done.
Then these sisters succeeded through battles hard-won.
And when your children dream of becoming a Knight.
Parents tell of these sisters who stood up to fight.

The Legend

Together they faced a thousand an one foes,
Against the usurpers they stood toe-to-toe.
The first of the seven was as strong as she was proud,
Her voice like a siren as she fought through the crowd.
She fought like a lion and killed without mercy,
Before her fierce roar, her enemies did flee.
With Krimzin in hand she fought and she died.
The Broadsword she'd wield, her emotions to hide.
"Please lay me down sister, upon my own shield,
My sword at my breast and Death at my heels.
My sisters stay strong, Goddess keep you secure.
Noble my death, and my Rebirth assured.
Thank Goddess our victories." Said the first, **Sister Seven,**

While starting down her road to the heavens…

> *The road the sisters take is long but it's true,*
> *The destination, though short, will return them to you.*
> *Give them thanks and ask them for boons*
> *As you look for them nightly through Artemis Moons.*

Clouds swallowed sky as the enemy drew near.
The six sisters left, their hearts absent of fear.
As the call comes upon them and these six go to war.
Honoring sister **Seven,** they battle still more.
As the enemy comes at them, **Sister Six** shows her might.
She raises her mace and grips her shield tight.
For **Sister Seven** and the loss of their lands
She leads the sisterhood, their lives in her hands.
Says the **Sixth** to the **Fifth. "***Die though I must,*
With honor I go and to you goes my trust.
I see sister **Seven***. She is waiting for me,*
To give my life for you, for **Four** *and the three."*
And although sister **Six** *had died before dawn,*
The sisters gave praise and then sang her Death Song.

> *The road the sisters take is long but it's true,*
> *A road meant for them, a road dared by few.*
> *Marching toward war, a sobering tune.*
> *As they carry it proudly 'neath Artemis moons*

Battles always rage, their duty never to end,
The Will of the Fates, doomed never to bend.
Five sisters go forth, swords and bows in their hands,
To seek out injustice come to threaten the land.
They leave none to escape, leave feasts for the crows.
Five faces her enemy, armed only with the bow.
"Artemis I call you, guide my arrow true,
Through Wolven, my bow, though arrows be few.
Come for me foul beasts! Come if you must!", she cries.

"But face death you will as my silver arrows fly!
My body is calm, my thoughts are yet poised,
Though you yell, shriek and curse, my mind absent of noise."
Overwhelmed though she was, **Five** fought to the last,
And looking to her sisters with a bellowing laugh, she said:

The road that I take is long but not new,
The destination is short and I will return to you.
Give me your blessing as I grant you this boon,
To look on you nightly from 'tween Artemis moons.

Four now are left who can answer the call,
For the three sisters they sadly watched fall.
With her great axe, the wildcat screams,
Showing the enemy what being a Valkyrie means.
"How many times," asks **Three** *"must we fight off this horde?"*
"Until none are left," answers **Four,** *"who can carry a sword!*
So join with me now and let us again march toward war!
Goddess grant us a victory, **Battle-Sisters** *once more!*
I have lived a full life, love and war with sisters,
I now join our dear **Seven**, *and for you I will kiss her!*
Cry though you will sisters, you know 'tis the debt.
A price we must pay, a price long ago set.
So turn not your eyes and watch me in glory,
As I die axe-in-hand and join in our story.

The road the sisters take is long but it's true,
The destination, though short, will return them to you.
Give them your thanks and ask them for boons
As you look for them nightly through Artemis Moons.

Three asks for little as she watches sister **Four** die,
"Except, my dear Goddess, let us dance 'cross the sky.
Someday I will join them and all will rejoice.
But not until this enemy's heard my battle-trained voice!
Bloodletter lashed out slicing an arc through the horde,

The Gods through her, released energy long-stored.
"My sisters and I carry swords and Valkyrie shields,
'Cross the great plains and battle-strewn fields.
With my two sisters, the only ones I have now,
Under sun we fight, sweat beading our brow.
Send me to Elysium with one parting kiss,
And know that there's nothing more noble than this:
To die for your sisters and watch 'cross the veil,
As one sister lives on to tell of our tale."

The road the sisters take is long but it's true,
The destination, though short, will return them to you.
Give them your thanks and ask them for boons
As you look for them nightly through Artemis moons.

Five are now gone and only two yet remain,
Watching five die these two bury their pain.
Two, she stands tall and holds her sword tight,
Showing enemies no fear and proving Valkyrie might.
Strategy is best with Athena by your side,
Two calls for her aid and again turns the tide.
With plenty of enemies, more to come on the morrow,
Valkyrie women fight proud and bury their sorrow.
Into the breach, these two rage 'gainst the lines,
They are fearsome and hungry and fighting for time.
Sister **One** falters and **Two** jumps to defend,
Saving her sister last of luck she does spend.
Two nods at her sibling and returns to the fray,
And although she did fall, **Two** carried the day.

The road the seven sisters walk is long but it ends,
The destination is short but returns them to friends.
To bask in War's glory and receive Victory's boon.
While constantly gazing between Artemis moons.

Now left is just **One,** and alone she does rise,
A lust for vengeance, death and blood in her eyes.
She casts off the shield that **Two** covered her with,
She is ready for death, her only reason to live.
Valkyrie-born, forged from ice and from fire,
Destined to join her sisters upon funeral pyre.
She grins at her foe, she dares them, *"Come closer!"*
The enemy pauses, for this enemy knows her.
With a swing of her sword, the enemy lines shatter,
The enemy army is now left in tatters.
There is a chill in the enemy, a cold fear at last,
For **One** becomes seven and chance of mercy has passed.
They run and they scream, a fierce and frightening sound,
As the last of their enemies at last are cut down.

Epilogue

Her wounds were too grievous, Athena's temple was saved,
Future Valkyrie women a road seven have paved.
To fight for their sisters, to the end if they must,
And to die sword-in-hand is the Valkyrie Trust.
Now these seven sisters shine down on us all,
Seven bright stars daring you to answer the call.

The road of the Seven Sister was long but goes on.
For if one still lives on, she will carry the song.
Honoring her sisters she will be seeing them soon.
And join in their brightness between Artemis moons.

The road of the Seven Sisters is a testament to you,
To reach for the stars and to sisterhood stay true.
Because sisters are everything, a blessing, a boon.
A gift seven have passed down from Artemis moons.

Sabine Valkyrie: Colonel - Nightshade Division

THE ROAD OF THE SEVEN SISTERS

BOOK III : BETWEEN A HAMMER AND AN ANVIL

The bow was one of the most magickal items she'd ever owned, gifted her when she was still young after the battle that lost their homeland. It was said to be built by the Gods Themselves, and although she loved to fancy that myth, she knew that it was not the Goddess Artemis, nor Her husband Apollo, but some of the greatest bowyers from Themis-Kyra, who in Clarissa's estimation were just as good. Even the Gods Themselves would have to admit this truth.

The wings were fashioned from the bones of an Eldarr Dragon named Fireclaw who'd died during the fall of the Amazonian isle and the handle that attached the wings was made from blood metal. It was strung with webbing called 'starlight' that came froma giant, magickal Sumarian spider in the desert lands of Ry'locke. Four rings controlled different powerful magicks that the bow possessed with a fifth that was ever-present and never needed the aid of the rings. This last was the production of magickal arrows that would appear when the bearer ran out of conventional ones. But these were limited to less than twenty per day before the magick was exhausted. In them was the power to hit any target no matter the distance or the obscuring of vision. The accuracy was extended even to the wooden-shafted arrows.

When the signal flags were raised Clarissa and the other archer captains, including Captain Darwazeh, gave the order. "Loose!" They yelled, almost in unison and thousands of shafts flew from their bows, arching their way toward the enemy. The front ranks of the usurper army raised their shields as missiles rained down upon them. The trolls and giants strained in rage against their chains as they were hit by dozens of shafts, as if being stung by thousands of wasps.

Overhead thunder boomed louder and within the clouds lightning began to lance unnaturally through them.

"Again!" Yelled Clarissa, "Loose!" She commanded, and this time as arrows rose, mages within the allied army added magickal fire that ignited the tips of them to rain fire upon the enemy. Where they struck, fire spread across the surface of the target because of the magick, unless warded against it.

Clarissa looked again into the sky to see that the bolts of lighting grew thicker and surged with a violent urgency. When she cast her gaze back to where Lana stood at the sacrificial fire, she could see that this uncanny storm in the midst of a winter day was the priestess's doing.

Lana stood before the massive bonfire, her arms raised toward the sky in supplication to the Gods, screaming for the soldiers who'd remained nearby to bring her more sacrifices. Her eyes glowed a bright violet as knights dragged thrashing green bodies over to the inferno and with the command from the warrior priestess tossed them unceremoniously into it, causing the fire to grow even higher and from within it a surge of electrical power flew skyward, exploding into the bolts that now raced across the darkened clouds.

A Sister's Lament

by Marlaya Morrowind

All my sisters are now dead
and I know that I am next
If my death would bring them back
My heart would no longer be vexed

I cry every night for my sisters
The torment, the pain, of their loss
although I accept that this is our fate
For glory and for fame their deaths cost

I look to those stars between moons
I watch for my sisters at night.
I call out to them and I cry
But always I keep them in sight.

They raised me and taught me to fight
A boon that I can never repay
But live for them I always will
And I will love for them every day

"Destiny never travels a straight road, though we must follow it nonetheless. No matter how crooked or difficult it becomes."

- Carya, the Angelic Oracle of Arkfall-

✦ 57 ✦

"The light shines for All but the Evil ones and their followers to see.

For they and their followers live in the Darkness of ignorance, knowing not the peace of Aten"

From the book of Aten – Book VIII
Chapter 7, Verse One

"Until I die I fight!"

THE SHADOW

by Marlaya Morrowind

The shadow of death lingers long
its fingers reach out from the dark
And its siren's call beckons to me
Death's bowyer, his arrow hits the mark

It hides away in the shadows
It waits for me in the deep
Its seductive song calls out to me
Calls me to the darkness of death's keep

SONG OF THE DREAMER / MARLAYA'S SONG

- written by Marlaya Morrowind

The Road

So I walk this road
My feet kissing the ground
and with every step
my heart had been found
The closer I come to it
to the place where I die
The longer this road seems to me
My old self, her body to lie

Sabine's Resistance

The Song of Resistance
Its melody moves through me
Coarsing through my thighs
it enlivens me and courage flies

It begins with the weight upon my heart
And my hard-heart does deny
I push, then I pull this love to me
Until to places uncharted I fly

Sirens of War

Responding to the horns of war
their blaring loud in our ears
we let down our hair and we fly
banishing all doubt and our fear

Sirens of battle they call us
Banshees of death at our best
Hear our screams as we call you
To deliver your soul to its rest

✦

HOUSE EVERSOAR

"We remain sharp as the steel we wield"

Liegehold: Their lands consist of the entirety of the area known as the Tail.

Capitol: DragonKnight Hall

Hair Colour: Blue **Eye Colour:** Purple

Dragon Claws: Cazna (midnight blue) and Adamon (Green)

Patron God/ess: Ares & Athena

Palladium: A sword inside a stone

<u>Primary Occupation:</u> Military, Knighthood

<u>Bannerhouses:</u> Falconcry, Brightfeather, Boulton, Turan, Pelion, Aptera, Vata, Zara, Sithonia, Grodur, Fulkrin, Berwick, Gurard, Dodona, Vili, Aeri, Connell (of Sga'na), Eldesmere, Honoura (of Tispak), Cumae, kitkis, Nazili, Tozi, Bradoke, Aitkens, Vikos, Eldunar, Manship (of Naousa), Zakyntos, Palmer (of Galudar Isle-Dheskati), Cazna (of Wood Valley), Sharp, Burns, Garvin, Croftward (bastards), Gortin, Reilley, Raymond

THE SEVEN DRAGONKNIGHT VIRTUES AND THEIR OATH OF SERVICE

"Be ashamed to die, oh knight, unless you do it whilst in service to the Crown and Her people, and ashamed once more if you die without a weapon in hand…"

~Dragonknight Nur-Isis Draclunari – 2E 970

There are seven Sacred Virtues of a Dragonknight and their Oaths, and these are:

1. Justice - 'With Justice we punish the evil and the wicked.'
2. Courage – 'With Courage we defend our Country and her people.'
3. Compassion – 'With Compassion we give and forgive those who are in need and deserving.'
4. Truth – 'With Truth we fight corruption, vice and the shadow.'
5. Strength – 'With Strength from the Gods we uphold the weak and the powerless.'
6. Wisdom – 'With Wisdom we give counsel to our Ladies and Lords, and future generations.'
7. Honor – 'With Honor we fulfill our oaths.'

The Seven Sisters and the Virtues:

1. Sabine – Justice
2. Camille – Courage
3. Clarissa – Compassion
4. Kiera – Truth
5. Lana – Strength
6. Athena – Wisdom
7. Marlaya – Honor

HOUSE EVERSOAR BATTLE HYMN

by Lord Storm Eversoar

March together on fields of war
never knowing what's in store
Eversoar, Everosar, Eversoar!

10,000 foes, we want more!
they'll all cower at our defening roar,
Eversoar, Eversoar, Eversoar!

Heroes of Ry'gel's Ancient Lore
The king and Queens, an oath we swore
Eversoar, Eversoar, Eversoar!

From Ry'gel, to the Isle of Ayerlore
we are warriors to our cores
Eversoar, Eversoar, Eversoar!

Wading through the blood and gore
Come on men! We shall endure
Eversoar, Eversoar, Eversoar!

Fighting unto distant shores
Tell me men what we fight for
Eversoar, Eversoar, Eversoar!

THE BLOODRYDERS' CHARGE

Beacons of hope we soar above, a terror in the skies
From scale and tooth to sword and shield
Dragonriders will fly

Through impossible odds we carry banners to war
Routing enemy with raging fire
Hear the Bloodryders roar.

Cover our allies with a fierce and terrible might
Sword and claw we draw blood
All will cower, dragonriders take flight

New riders tested, the war horns announce the call to arms
Surrendering to no one
Bloodryders, like hornets will swarm

A bane to the hordes, cowering 'neath our wings
triumphant are the Bloodryders
As the enemy feels our sting

Smoke fills the air and the enemy calls their retreat
Stand proudly brave riders
As our enemy faces defeat

When smoke clears and retire we from our last fight
Victors we are still vigilant
And when called, again we take flight.

Failure we shall never know if but one lives to heed the call
Valour is our choice
For we are Bloodryders ALL – hu-ah!

A'lonna Ravencrest and Mjendor Alonnasteed

LAST WRITINGS OF APOLLONIUS SICARIUS

It is the three thousand, two-hundred and thirtieth year of the 6th Era of the Aldari and I have just received news of the passing of my twin sister and the greatest Queen of Ry'gel here to fore known, Star Sicarius. The Priests say that she died in her sleep but I am ever of a suspicious mind and I believe it to have been something far more sinister. Of course, Lucius and the other mages of his rank would say that I've gone 'round the bend,' jumping at shadows and all of that. But I know what I know and few know what I do.

The visions come daily and it is all that I can do to sift through them like ashes after a fire to find a piece of threat that will reveal the answers that I seek. I see a Doom rising upon the horizon. Of course, mine own sun will set long before that Time. Gods be merciful, I hope I am gone then.

I do not envy those who will live in the Times of the Oath. Even now, Wilds ravage the land, lawless beasts and men who go unchecked making travel precarious at best.

Oh! The visions! A plague to my soul and my existence! Soon I pray, I shall be taken into the Cycle of Immortality so I might be rid of this curse once and for all. Perhaps the Gods and Fates shall deem my service worth respite and give my next life to one of at least moderate tranquility. Even now the visions burn their gruesome sights into my brain and even with a life tranquil and serene next, I fear I shall be scarred with them for my soul's eternity.

There shall come a Time when blood shall flow from brave Elven warriors like rivers from the mountains and their melting snows. Demons will invade and Gods will rise, while the Titans re-awaken to claim Their stolen worlds.

Indeed! We shall not even see them coming.

A disease plagues the land even now, unchecked by all but a few. Beware the Dark Command of Chaos and Her minions. There are Oaths and then there are OATHS. There is the ONE, and then there are the many. Ask not what the Time of the Oath is, but instead what it will bring. By fulfilling the Oath and the oaths you shall destroy the Worlds. Destroy, but not send to the void. Through Death comes New Life, not unlike the Great Phoenix, a bird of fire that means Change and Resilience.

Storms from the Gods will unleash starvation and will bring forth war. You will live in despair and in confusion and your children will fight each other for right and for wrong.

From whence does Hope arise? Where will she be born and whom shall her parents be? I wonder. Commoners? Royalty? Or even Divinity. Perhaps all three…

But listen to this! - Students of Prophecy – She shall be born and overlooked. But life around Her shall forever be altered. The Gods shall hearken to Her birth, the Heiress of Proxima to sit Hera's Throne, and a new Beacon will arise to call the Titan's return.

You shall be alone, and yet she will be among you. She will travel alongside Proxima's greatest hero, under noses of adept and the Divine. But she shall know one of the Greater lessons and it is this: When a prairie fire threatens, best not to run from it lest you be overrun and consumed. Instead run towards and through it. You will be burned… but you will be alive, and you will soar with Gods.

Hope will merge with despair and Together like Fire and Ice, its steam will become an Eclipse of all that existed before. Through Darkness will come the blinding light of Victory, Encircling, Darkness will be that light.

TIME OF THE OATH PROPHECY BY APOLLONIUS SICARIUS

'Listen well Children, and hear of the Oath,

When the Time as Promised comes at last
The Time of the Veil, the mold is cast.
Divine Direction in Ry'gel's Hist'ry
Divine the Past, solves the Myst'ry

Pretenders will reign with false claims
Stealing Rule through Prince's shame
Seek the heir who'll hide no more
Even the odds and settle a score

In the tomb, Brontur's victims reside
Find the grave, Spirit will guide
To save Ry'gel, the waiting Lady Seek
Seen thru book from which Goddess speaks

In a Circle of Fire on warm spring Night
Fated Child of the Oath, sealed by candlelight
A king's sacrifice secures the Royal Line
Child of Oath born to do what's divined

A time of chaos begins in Times of despair
Secret of Kings at last is laid bared
Dest'ny shall move hearts 'cross the land
to Awaken Prophecy Great Warriors must stand.'

HOUSE JUNEAU (JUNO)

"It Surrounds us, it flows through us, it binds us"

Liegehold: From the Thurber lands in the North, to the Annwin Lands in the South. From the Enceladean Sea and Dragonflame Islands to Dragonwing Bay

Capitol: Aetherhall

Hair Colour: Purple   **Eye Colour:** Purple

Dragonclaws: Azazel (min) Purple Venator (Nightsun) Black

Patron God/ess: Aradia, Hekate, Isis, Thoth, Hermes

<u>Palladium:</u> Nude statue of Isis, w/horn & disc headdress and wings straight out.

<u>Primary Occupations:</u> Mages, Sorcerers, Pneumenonic Sciences, Education, Scholors

<u>Bannerhouses:</u> Briarwood, Vulcanis, Centares, Hoderra, Sicarius, Lorne, Paliden, Sundown, Laird, Atlantis, Nettlesbane, Circinus, Calledin, Eversmith, Aldran, Epona, Gareint, Garret, Isis, Alvirus, Amut, Hearthstone, Leilanni, Silvanus, Ezran, Corvus, Coldburn, Crozier, Wittans, Wicce, Croftwards (bastards). Mikkol, Mudgett (Magi), Lemue

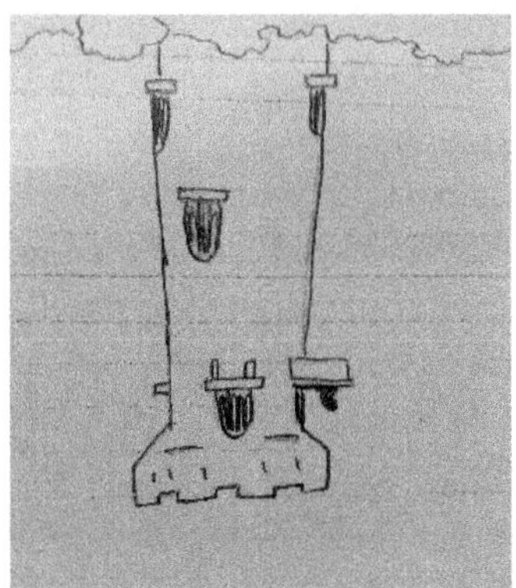

TIME OF THE OATH CHRONICLES

"You fly really well," Myrflor commented, evoking a broad, proud smile from the elder mage.

"Why thank you my dear," Lucius responded, releasing his grip upon the Captain's wheel and giving her an embellished diving swan bow.

"Did you hear that Ven?" He asked to the dragon above them. "The young squire said that I fly well."

"Please don't encourage him Myrflor." Said Venator, his grip tightening upon the handles of the large carrying basket.

"How long before we get there?" Asked A'lonna,

"not long, not long." Replied the mage, still pretending to steer the great wheel in front of him. Pointing ahead and slightly higher than they, he said, "Look, we are almost there."

The passengers noticed suddenly, a large island floating before them. Like it had been plucked straight from the sea they could see it appearing from behind some magickal veil, great mountains creating its rim on the top of the island and craterous and jagged rocks below. And at its center extending down toward the sea, which lay miles below, was a long cylindrical tower. The island itself could have fit an entire liege-hold and the tower was as big as one of the keeps at Ravencrown.

"It is over 150 miles long and at least three-quarters that in width". He said as if reading their thoughts. "And see there, just underneath." He pointed to the tower. "That is my home."

"Our home," Corrected the black dragon from above with an annoyed sigh.

"Yes, yes, of course," Lucius responded just as annoyed.

"But…" Myrflor stammered. "It is upside down!"

"Why yes my dear." Replied the mage. "Yes it is…."

Words and Thoughts of Words

Words and thoughts of words – come from somewhere
Destroying and making true what is otherwise fiction
Giving away and taking what is needed from around them
Writers and readers, interpreting different things
Watching and waiting for the other ball to drop
But still the words finding meaning from the story
Leaving one to wonder – where do I begin?

Orcs

What is it about orcs?
For one they are extremely rude
But what makes them interesting?
Perhaps it is the way they kill?

The Cage

I am more than just a man in a box
My walls are not walls, my bars are not bars
In the choices I make and the thoughts my own
Where are walls that contain what can not be
maybe if I looked where you are I would find them

Cycle of Mortality

I lost you in a Season's fog of War
But you'll forever be with me in my heart
Don't really know how or if I'll ever love again
Nor how I'll be able to make a new start

Give me time Life, before you ask it of me
I am just a traveler in the Cycle of Mortality
I've died and died to return again
And I've already forgotten where I've been

How many times should I have to endure this?
Before I can call it quits, call it the end.
My heart seems so fragile, ready to explode
you were the only one on whom I could depend

Give me time Life, before you make me start over
My heart it hurts and will not give rest
I'm still recovering from the loss of a lover
Tell me ye Gods, is this some sort of test?

Your eyes were filled with such life and hope
How could I know you would leave so soon
I would give anything to see you again
Oh Gods, please, I beg you to grant me this boon

Give me time Life, so that I can catch my breath
My heart's been torn in two and without mend
I've only just started to deal with this death
A deep, dark void is where it's been sent

Perhaps it seems selfish to you, that I still mourn
But what know ye Gods of love true and fleeting?
Your love is eternal and never will it be lost
For your love resides not in a heart that is beating.

It is in-Time child, we give you love that is fleeting
But we give love again to many hearts still beating
you'll see your love again, if truly fated to be
Be wise and be patient, and wait the cycle of mortality.

My Mother's Ancestors

My mother's ancestors watch over me
Blessing my feet, my womb and my heart
My mother's ancestors made me who I am
And it is to them that I am a part

Their blood it courses through me
Carrying with it the secrets of their past
I am the child of my mother's mother
and through my children our bloodline shall last

-Marlaya Morrowind

Fate Alone

We create our own destiny, create our own life
We bring forth our everyday with fervent hope
To watch on the sidelines we miss the blessing
of experience and increasingly steep is this slope

Fates they can rule us, their laws never to bend
But the day's joys and pains are ours to own
Give in to Them and hand your lives over to Gods
For in this you are assured to never be alone

The Oracle: Kianna Nightstar

The Goddess Aradia

House Silvermane

"When all others fall, Silvermane standards remain tall."

Liegehold: From the Borders of Arachne Lands in the west to the Olympian Sea in the east and from the Lands of Raventhrone in the North to the Lands of Avarin in the south.

Capitol: Fox Hall

Hair Color: Silver   **Eye Colour:** Indigo

Dragonclaws: Xanon (White) and Averon (Silver)

Patron God/ess: Epona, Aesclepius, panacea, Hygeia and Apollo

Palladium: Winged Pegasus

Primary Occupation: Health, Clerics, Horse/Pegasii trainers, Heralds, Standard-bearers

Bannerhouses: Rhoden, Hovereye (of Lakeview), Ivalite, Narcissa, Canes, Anaris, Circe, Darma, Pyrochlore, Burnhold, Ulor (Of Manortown), Bernal, Feefall, Skara Brae, Palon, Maldon, Rivermarch, Magnis, Morningstar, Hydrus, Orta, Paros, Almiras, Octans, Elevsis, Titan, Flulia, Roons, Croftwards (bastards), Ossgud

HOUSE GRYFFYN

"Pride, Excellence & Honour"

Liegehold: The Region known as Elvenheart, or Elvenhold. North-South from Astokes (N) to Southwatch. East-West from West Coast to Astan in the East.

Capitol: Loftwing Eyerie

Hair Colour: White   **Eye Colour:** Amethyst (Purple)

*Note: House Gryffin does not have any dragon claws because their sole focus is on raising, training and riding griffins.

Patron God/ess: Apollo

<u>Palladium:</u> Apollo's chariot being pulled by a griffins

<u>Primary Occupation:</u> Griffin Breeders, Trainers & Riders ; Couriers/Messengers ; Recon.

<u>Bannerhouses</u>: Albirus, Nesu, Elvenheart, Pomona, Pothos, Kore, Thera, Tirane, Psarion, Furig, Astan, Truesong, Luringheart (Dale), Roman (Romulus), Florina, Scylla, Kozani, Alya, Bolduc, Sutani, Hirole, Gracchus, Beaton, Nuri, Iraklion, Dragonbane, Pythea, Titan, Lacon, Araneus, Lethe, Astakos, Delos, Chalcis, Kankali, Eretria, Pisodos, Naxplion, Nahi, Varus, Maretta, Leonidas, Cepheus, Europa, Servia, Aetius, Croftwards (bastards), Nadoo

HOUSE THURBER

"With Rule, rod & Compass, we build Kingdoms"

Liegehold: The Crown in the Northern most west to the South at the lands of House Juneau (Juno). East it meets the top of Dragonwing Bay and in the West the Enceladean Ocean.

Capitol: Siege Hall

Hair Colour: Salmon **Eye Colour:** Violet

Dragon Claws: Nagast (Pink) Adamon (Wilder) Green Forest

Patron God/ess: Ptah, Hephaestos

<u>Palladium</u>: A compass upon an Anvil

<u>Primary Occupations</u>: Blacksmiths, builders, masons, Architects.

<u>Bannerhouses</u>: Eguus, Mirbolt, Akrona, Artan, Petrocos, Acrisius, Riticulus, Grusha, Allatu, Amphion, Graccha, Pharat, Mare, Maelgwyn, Fjaniir, Dolmar, Houhet, Vulcanis, Ammut, Slepnir, Crona, Lana, Halron, Varkun, Epidaurus, Maester, Mallister, Journeyman, Waddell, Coalburn, Fuller, Mason, Croftward (bastards), Steadyhand.

HOUSE ARACHNEA

"The Web Connects us all...."

Liegehold: Form the North the lands of Arachnea touch the southern border of Raventhrone at the Bedwyr mts. In the southern lands abut House Gryffin.. In the West they extend from the Neck Canal and Western Ocean to the lands of Silvermane in the East.

Capitol: Widow's Keep

Hair Colour: Orange   **Eye Colour:** Violet

Dragon Claws: Xaxos (orange) and Radmon (brass)

<u>Patron God/ess</u>: Arachne, Athena, Hera

<u>Palladium</u>: Crystal Spider with the naked top of a woman extending from body.

<u>Primary Occupations</u>: Textiles, skilled labour, clothing. Linen, Historians

<u>Bannerhouses</u>: Altair, Avons, Caden, Dracon, Astoreth, Pagani, Wulf, Aridh, Grevena, Locana, Agrippa, Aradia, Elea, Bolduc, Cyme, Agraffa, Ermoupoli, Athos, Asha, Larel, Florens, Venatici, Feeney, Heany, Heady, Riddel, Dyeman, Dorsey, Ridley, Fossell, Croftward (bastards), Moroe, Watsin

MY ENEMY, MY LOVE/OR THE FLAGS OF OUR HEARTS

We were bred under different banners
We were raised in different lands
By sword and by shield we have lived
But now we join roads we've joined hands

Your words are a boon to my heart
Where once you were enemy to me
I will live what is left next to you
Never again apart will we be

Our banner is now one and the same
The flags of our hearts now combined
my heart is yours for the taking
and your heart, once resistant, now mine.

DRAGON & RIDERS' LAMENT

Don't go….
We are a team – I am yours and you are mine
Feels like we've had so little time.

Don't go….
Hold onto our love so we soar into the sky
now that you are gone, how can I fly

Please…. Don't go
you are my world, and have been my friend
my heart cries out for the pain to end

Don't let go….
Why have you vanished and left me alone
Our soaring love has fallen like a stone

you don't have to go….
You could stay just a little while longer
At least until my heart grows stronger

I don't want you to leave….
How can I go on without you here in my embrace
It is a future I've always been unwilling to face

you don't know….
What I would give to see you, hear you again
I will love you forever, and forever be your friend

Promise to remember….
No matter where you go, I will always have you
you will always have my heart and it is always true

And yet….
If you loved me, then why did you leave me
now my soul cries out, can you hear its scream?

One step closer….
When I call out to you, can you hear your name
or is my voice unheard, is it all in vain

Can I say….
That I would for sake all others and the Gods to hold on
Without you by my side, I don't know how to be stronger

I'll let go….
If I must I will, if only to allow you to be free
As long as you realize what it is you mean to me
you can go…. Please go now…
Be still my heart and please still your voice
though it is hard to endure, this is my choice.

HOUSE ANNWIN

"We Know"

Liegehold: House Annwin Territory extends from the Western Ocean (Enceladean Ocean) to the Necklace Canal (East). Its Northern border abuts House Juneau, south to the sea

Capitol: Warden Hall

Hair Colour: Tan/Sand   **Eye Colour:** Purple

Dragonclaws: Adamon (Emerald) and Mors Ultor (Tan/Brown)

Patron God/ess: Hermes/Thoth

<u>Palladium:</u> Ranger sits upon a rock with a book in his/her lap. An owl sits upon his shoulder and one hand clutches a scroll.

<u>Primary Occupations:</u> Rangers, Intelligence, Spies and Specialized Courier Services. Advisors to King/Queens, Lords/Ladies, ETC. Home of the Shadow Guild.

<u>Bannerhouses</u>: Auron, Hartshorn, Morfans, Andros, Redmarsh, Brochvael, Sagramoor, Arjunna, Hellid, Coalster, Lyria, Talon, Alnar, Solon, Celwin, Dengus, Edhessa, Miriam, Egres, Bell, Sparti, Kifisia, Kaliya, Arynn, Cairn, Hunter, Breault, Croftword (bastards), Fortier

Reilanna Snakeroot – doodle by Keith Morrissette

THE ROAD OF THE SEVEN SISTERS
BOOK III: BETWEEN A HAMMER AND AN ANVIL

CHAPTER 7

"Good, now go." Clarissa responded. "They're almost upon us. We'll give you a head start."

"But…" Marlaya hesitated. "Come with us Clarissa." She said, grabbing the sister's arm.

Clarissa embraced Marlaya suddenly. "Go. I'll catch up." She said to her and then pushed her away. "Your sister would kill me if I didn't see you safely away." She told her with a tense smile.

"Now go!"

Marlaya, with Captains Croteau and Darwazeh and the nine House Guard belonging to the Lady-Princess headed back toward the tent that was already being dismantled by camp squires and Emillar's ladies-in-wait. Nearby the sleigh awaited her and with it were the horses for the House Guard as well as Marlaya's own horse, *Windswift.*

Captain Darwazeh climbed into the carriage with Emmilar, and Matthew and Marlaya mounted their horses. In moments the sleigh was being pulled forward by its eight large horses. From behind Marlaya could hear the sound of battle engaging as swords clashed and men and women yelled or screamed.

The blizzard was heavy and snow whipped at their faces but Marlaya wasn't cold. Bloodmetal armor was good for that. It's magick was warm and along with being light and yet extremely hard, it was excellent for all weather.

Altogether, Emillar's protective entourage consisted of no more than sixty people, including twenty of her Household retainers. If they were attacked now by any number of enemy over the forty who were knights with them, they would be fighting their last and House Thurber would die here in the snow-driven plains of Equus.

But, although the Gods can be prodigal in their aid and allegiances, the Fates are down-right fickle. For as this retreating troupe made their way as speedily as they could deep into Equus Plains toward the ships that brought the Nightshade Division here, there came howls from behind. At first when Marlaya looked she could see nothing through the driving snow. But soon, shapes began to appear and Windswift joined by the Lady-Princess's own horse that Marlaya towed began to nicker and whine frantically.

Looking back again Marrlaya saw the giant direwolves that carried their Naglari and goblin riders.

"Company!" Yelled Matthew to the Lady-Princess's Homeguard. With the snow, some did not hear him. But those who did started looking behind to see the danger. Now more than twenty wolf-riders had caught up to the Lady-Princess's entourage.

"Company!" He yelled again. "Defense!"

More than thirty of the Home guard slowed, allowing the wolf-riders to draw near. Marlaya and Matthew did the same, and already *Shatter* was in her hand and raised. A wolf rider caught up to her, his steed slavering and growling, nipping at Windswift's flanks, To the horse's credit he did not panic, but instead moved into the other animal.

A Direwolf is big, almost the size of a horse, and far quicker and agile. But an eponodari is smarter and sentient. Which means that it can think much like an elf or a dwarf. With his armour of bloodmetal, the wolf would have a hard time getting its jaws into the horse's flesh, and Windswift knew that.

This would give Marlaya an advantage, allowing her to maneuver in her saddle and swing at her opponent without either the rider or his wolf to take the horse down. And Marlaya used this to hack at the exposed wolf who veered away in response, and then came back in again.

Ahead, the sleigh had picked up speed but was being chased by three wolf riders who were already overcoming the guards who remained with it. Marlaya needed to get to the Lady-Princess. Granted, Captain Darwazeh was inside the cabin with her, but if she were outnumbered…

Marlaya thrust Shatter into the neck of the wolf and with a yelp of pain the wolf began to falter, but not before the goblin rider on its back lunged for Marlaya almost knocking her from Windswift's back. And as the wolf fell away, the tiny green warrior snapped his own jaws at Marlaya's helmeted face. With Shatter in one hand, she battered the goblin's face while holding him back with the other. It was all that she could do to get him off of her when he suddenly stopped, his growls turning to bubbling chokes as Marlaya saw a spearhead protruding through his neck.

Matthew had come alongside at that moment and speared the little green creature. But just as he was pulling it from the gullet of the goblin there came a whinny of panic from horses nearby. To their horror, they were riding straight past the sleigh as it came slamming into the backside of its dying horses and flipping over in a spray of snow and ice to rest, overturned, on its side.

Both Marlaya and Matthew steered their horses back to the scene, but before Marlaya could get near it something knocked she and her horse sideays into a snowdrift. Marlaya panicked and trying to dig her way frantically from the snow, she could hear the dying screams of Windswift as he was being torn apart by a giant direwolf. When she emerged from the snowbank, Shatter still in her hand, she could see the dire wolf, Windswift's throat still in its jaws as it looked back at her, its eyes feral and hungry.

Turning toward her, the wolf stalked her way and Marlaya stood defiantly, sword poised to meet it.

HOUSE DRACLUNARI

"Like the Gods, Gold runs through our veins…."

Liegehold: From the Northernmost arch of the Crescent Mountains abutting both Gryffyn and Avarin Thrones, to the South at the claw in the Gulf of the Moon. From the Lands of Gryffyn and Feeding Plains in the West to Avarin Lands in East.

Capitol: Mistgate

Hair Colour: Gold   **Eye Colour:** Indigo

Dragon Claws: Belial (Gold) and Mars Ultor (Brown).

Patron God/ess: Ra, Hermes, Pan

<u>Palladium</u>: A golden wyvern made of crystal

<u>Primary Occupations</u>: Trade, Currency, Merchant, Markets

<u>Bannerhouses</u>: Astan, Minaret, Faraday, Arfedson, Cephei, Ultor, Pahank, Fomal, Senyx, Khorax, Platres, Duilman, Rothgar, Echbel, Sankari, Dagdolur, Lirus, Wyvern, Croftward (bastards).

SABINE

How would I describe my lovely and powerful Sabine
Should it be in the way that her sword swings with her hips
or maybe it should be in the way that her body is ever lean
Her skin soft and smooth between my fingertips

When the call comes upon her and she stands tall and fierce
I look on with excitement as she raises her blade
Best when surrounded the enemy she will pierce
and with her strike to death the enemy she doth bade

Still you see, it's more than her kiss I receive at night
or the lure of her breasts in my hands that I crave
Nor her arms strong and true that cling to me tight
But maybe the memory of her fierce eyes that I save

But truly my friends it is her roar that sets my heart aflame
In bed or on field, love and war for her are just a game.

HOUSE KETO

"Our ships, our will, outlast even Poseidon's Waves!"

Liegehold: From the Asga'ardian Ocean in the North to the borders of Raventhrone and from Dragonwing Bay in the West to the Olympian Ocean in the East.

Capitol: Krakken's Keep

Hair Colour: Gray

Eye Colour: Violet

Dragonclaws: Stormchaser (Gray)

Patron God/ess: Poseidon, Triton & Amphitrite

<u>Palladium</u>: Trireme with a ram's head at its prow and giant tentacles as oars.

<u>Primary Occupation</u>: Shipwrights, Seamen (Women), Navy, Fishermen

<u>Bannerhouses</u>: Shalerite, Corkahn, Gorgon, Boulton, Dreadfort, Miren (N.), Lys, Burray, Bunnel, tokanar, Nera, Carina, Artemis, Antila, Ubbe, Arran, Skarr, Alanon, Waise, Tyrloris, Sevigg, Langur, Vela, Aquilus, Faireye, Feldspur, Wyvern, Krakken, Odysseus, Helmsman (Helm), Washburn, Portman, Dugan, Dowds, Gillespie, Croftwards (bastards), Manship

HOUSE AVARIN

"Refined Elegance, Grace, Honour, Nobility"

Liegehold: From the Silvermane Lands and Olympian Sea in the North, to the Tail and the Gulf of the moon in the South. From Draclunari Lands in West to the Olympian Sea in East.

Capitol: Winekeep

Hair Colour: Red   **Eye Colour:** Purple

Dragonclaws: Nagast (Red) and Xanon (Pearl)

Patron God/ess: Dionysus and Bacchus, Demeter and Kore

<u>Palladium</u>: Crystal Wine cup (Red)

<u>Primary Occupations</u>: Argiculture, Horticulture, Vitnters, Tree farmers.

<u>Bannerhouses</u>: Morgan, Dagres, Baela, Nalaxos, Eldis, Varlonn, Wyllda, Vine, Sprigga, Oak, Elm, Bannock, Falas/Arna, Crangr, Braxos, Fyr, Orda, Belathora, Serpena, Tiamat, Theban, Acus, Ryngar, Lydia, Minaret, Varkiza, Syros, Sustros, Zalamoxis, Pericles, Arilyn, Selene, Larsell, Duran, Briseis, Barton, Collins, Anders, Cook, Brown, Croftward (bastards), Cote (bee keepers).

THE COMING OF LUK'KHEN & THE ASGA'RD

-as told by the village elders of the Aesir

In ancient times on the planet of Proxima, in an icy region called Nordlund, the Asga'ard were still unknown and only the nord-goethir, or Nord Gods lived alone and isolated from the rest of the world. In the southern lands of Morgos and Enceladus, and other warmer regions lived all of the other Gods. The southern gods had created for themselves mortals that they could share the world with, and for the Ventergrada, the Winter Father Odhinn this was an insult.

"Why do our cousins need these mortals? The planet was given us by his Father Kronion." Odhinn complained. But His brother, the wise Freyr explained to Him that this showed wisdom on Zeus's part, because now there were mortals who worshipped and gave to He and the other Gods sacrifices, which increased Their power.

"Then should we not have our own mortals?" Asked Odhinn.

"We should indeed brother." Agreed Freyr. "But the secret to Life was only given to Ra and His Daughter Isis." Seeing that this had only angered Odhinn, Freyr quicky devised a solution and suggested it to His brother. "Perhaps brother, if we were to steal some of their mortals we could mate with them and then gift them with powers from each of us in order to make them superior to all others."

Odhinn was not entirely excited by this plan, but with little other options to gain His own mortals, He agreed, sending His sons Thorr and Baldur to raid the southern lands and bring back mortals. Upon the Return of the Divine brothers, they had with them hundreds of mortals from both the human and the dwarven stock.

"First," suggested Freyr, "We shall mate the human with the dwarf. Then, we will mate with what results."

Years later would bring the new race of the Aesir. Odhinn was very pleased and when it was done, each of the Ventergoethir gifted the Aesir with divine traits. All but two gave of Themselves, holding out Their powers divine from the mortals. Thorr and His adoptive brother Luk'khen refused to give away that which was a part of Themselves.

But it did not matter, for the Aesir were mighty enough indeed, and even the southern Gods were impressed by the innovation. But it had depleted the Goethir-nords and They would need to slumber for a time to regain strength. But first, before They could, They needed to teach the Aesir to live in the Northern land's harsh environment, and to use their Divine gifts to better their country and themselves.

Much to the delight of the Goethirnord, the Aesir adapted well to the land and its harsh climate, and even harsher beasts. Villages grew and tribes hived off of one another- each with its own Tavroda, or chief, Jarl and Ogghum. These were chiefs in their own right, the three that would govern each of the tribes. The Mother Chief came first, then the clan chief, and last the Holy man and/or woman. But when there were many clans and more tribes, the ventergoethir knew the Aesir would need a king, like Odhinn, so They appointed for them, a Venterken, or Winter-King.

Eventually the Ventergoethir needed to slumber and They were seen no more. Only Thorr could be seen once in awhile wandering the landscape until not even He was seen. But the people prospered and the bounties of the land were plentiful. The people were happy, and the tribes got along, trading during the warmer months, which were not exactly warm, but when the blizzards were less likely to come. During these times of trading the people would create games for competition, allowing clans and tribes to compete against one another for prizes. Marriages, and the promises of future marriages were made, and life was good.

But the land would not remain favorable to these Aesir, and it came one year that the northern country saw its first hardship. There was a blizzard that took many lives, coming during the times when winter storms did not come, and catching many unawares. It was followed by many more, and soon the Aesir were calling out to the the Goethir for help. Only one responded. He was one whom the people had never met before, one that the Aesir had been told thought Himself too good for them. But here He was, riding upon a giant sleigh through the blizzards, pulled by sixteen Andaralk. He called himself Luk'Khen.

Luk'khen offered to the people the help that they were begging for. When asked where the Goethir were, He explained that They had gone to the lands far in the south and had gotten Themselves captured by the southern Gods and the Elves there. The news scandalized the Aesir. Why would the southern Gods and Their people imprison the Goethir? They asked? Luk'Khen explained that it was to pay for the crimes the Goethir had committed in creating the Aesir.

"Listen to me Aesir," He said to the people. "You must build ships and travel to the lands of the Elves. You must take revenge for your Gods, and you must free Them from Their bondage. Not only this, but in the Elven lands are riches that you have never even dreamed of. The gods there have not only given to them fairer weather, but gifted them the materials to create weapons and hunting tools far superior to any other. And the gold that you covet? They have more than you have ever seen!"

There were those amongst the Aesir that were wiser than the other. One such was their own Venterken, who had inherited his kingship from his Uncle Wodhann. His name was Tristann, and he was not only wise, but a giant of a man and strong, some said, as Baldur Himself. He rode astride a giant ventercut, a tiger-like cat that had white fur with red stripes. Tristann did not trust the words of Luk'khen, although he had no real excuse as to why. Something in what the God said was wrong, and he could just feel it.

"Our people have never known war." He said, addressing the people and ignoring the goethir. "And from what the Venter-goethir have told us in the past, we want nothing of it. They place us here to keep us far away from the warring men of the south and their war goethir. What need have we of these riches that Luk'khen speaks of?"

"But they have our Gods!" Cried one of the hunters.

"Yes King Tristann, they have our Gods. They insult us by holding the Ventergoethir captive." Came another voice, this one from one of the Jarls. His name was Morfanns Vok Sleighir. He was leader of the Aesir in the south Nord lands of Val'hall, and had ever been in competition with Tristann, even claiming while drunk that he would make a far better Venterken.

Finally, Luk'khen stepped forward, his blue skin and white hairy body much resembling the harsh landscape around them. "Indeed. What need have you for the riches of the south? And I can see the doubt in your king's eyes that the Goethir, my broth-ers and sisters have been taken prisoner. Why wouldn't he doubt? They are Gods!" He looked at each of them, and finally to the Venterken and to Jarl Morfanns. "But I tell you true. They are captive and only you, their children can rescue Them. I alone can not do this because I am of the North even more than my own Goethirnorda. And Thorr, He is too drunk in His great mead hall to rescue them."

"Luk'Khen is a liar." Said Tristann, challenging the Venter gi-ant. "He would deceive us toward His own end."

"And what end is that, Tristann?" Asked Morfans.

"He is jealous of us."

All around them the people cried out in dismay, afraid that their king had just doomed them all. But Luk'khen only smiled and looked at the Venterkhen. "Tell me oh king, why would I be jealous of mortals?"

"Because Odhinn loves us more. And because He made all of you give of your powers to make us. And I think that this makes you jealous and scared."

Luk'khen laughed heartily. "Well, you are entertaining, I will give you this. But you are misguided. And I do not know where this hostility toward me comes from. I have come to give succor to your people who are suffering. Did I not bring gifts to see you through the winter? And did I not make the blizzard come to an end? You say that Odhinn loves you so much, but when He and the Goethir woke from their slumber, did They come to visit Their people the Aesir before trekking south to enjoy warmer climes and feast on the southern food, and make merry with the Elves? They did I tell you!" He thrust a finger into the air, and then pointed it at all of the people. "They did this and forgot about you here in the north. It was then that the Olympians laid Their trap for the Goethir. They imprisoned Them and now they hold Them as their entertainment in their great mead hall on a mountain."

"So it is that you want us to not only wage war with these Elves, but with their Gods as well." Said Tristann. "You said yourself, the Elves have poweful magick weapons, and they have been warring far longer than we of the Aesir. And what do we know of waging war with either they or the Gods?"

"I will teach you." Replied Luk'khen. "And make no mistake Venter-ken, eventually, if you have not gone to them first, the Elves and their allies will find you here in the north, and they will wage war with you. They will take your precious Nordlund, your wives and your children, and when they have whelped babies on them, they will have stolen even the mighty gifts that Odhinn Ventergrada gave to you."

"I do not doubt Luk'Khen's words." Jarl Morfanns announced to the people. "I will listen to Him and I will goto the southern lands to avenge our Gods!" Many around them cheered, but Tristann only shook his head in disgust. He knew that Luk'khen had deceived the people and had poisoned them to this purpose, although he had to admit that he could not know why he believed this. He had no proof, and he had nothing to reference the goethir's trickery. But the Venterken was wise, and there were still those who would listen to him.

"You say that we must build ships." Said Tristann. "You will not take wood from the Cweord to do this. And we have the most wilderness in all of Asga'ard. I and my clan will not help you."

"You would refuse aid to our Gods." Challenged Morfanns.

Tristann shook his head and nodded toward Luk'khen. "I would refuse aid to THIS god, if a god is what he is…" The Venterken spat. Disgusted and followed by more than seven tribes of the Aesir, those who came from the northwest of Asga'ard in the land of Cweord, Tristann turned and left the counsel of Luk'khen to return home.

Placing a hand of reassurance on the shoulder of Morfanns, the venter giant said, "Do not worry, you shall have wood for your ships. And it will be magickal wood, like none you have ever seen!"

It would be over two hundred years before the People who followed Morfanns returned. There had been more than twenty tribes, 40,000 Aesir who had gone with him. And when they rerturned they came ashore in the northlands of Asga'ard like a tidal wave. Since they had been gone, the Venterken had seized their lands and those they'd left behind, since there were none to care for them. The people who populated Val'hal did not recognize the people of Morfanns, who had once been their people, and sought to defend themselves against this seemingly foreign invader.

In the lands to the south, The people of Morfanns, now led by a man whose name was Vulnkengarr, the son of Morfanns looked darker, had become larger and there was a lust in their eyes, and a constant anger. They sought to claim Val'hal, saying that it was theirs by right. But the citizens of Val'hal instead called for the very aged Venterken, Tristann and his son Bjorn.

Those who had returned, their descendants were very much different than those who had left, now numbered in the hundreds of thousands. Without the Venterken and the people of Cweord, the citizens of Val'hal would surely be overrrun. And when the Venterken heard of the threats to the people of Val'hal, the aged king climbed the back of his ventercut and with 25000 warriors at their backs rode to meet these invaders.

When the two armies met on the plains of midgard, it was clear that the Venterken and his warriors were outnumbered. But he met with the leader of these new people that dared call themselves Asga'ardian. Vulnkengarr was a giant of a man, and he wielded a mighty battleaxe made from a metal unknown to the Aesir, a spoil no doubt from his raids of the south.

Although Tristann was greatly outnumbered he and his sons faced the enemy without fear. Vulnkengarr rode a giant direwolf named Fenrir and was accompanied by his daughter Hella. Both armies charged into battle without so much of a word to the other and it wasn't long before the old king Tristann was taken from the back of his Ventercut both he and his cat were torn apart by the mighty direwolf. Enraged, the Aesir Bjorn cried, "Vikingald!" and attacked Vulnkengarr. Praying to the God Thorr, Bjorn leapt upon the direwolf with his fathers battleaxe. Cutting the beast's shoulder before leaping away. When Vulkengarr fell from the back of his own mount, Bjorn was fast to take up the advantage, while Hella fought to get her to father in time.

None like to be bothered after a long night of drinking and merry making, but the fierce noise of battle woke the goethir from His slumber. Nursing a raging hangover, the God was none to happy to be interrupted and so rudely awakened. Swinging his great hammer, Mjolnir, Thorr jumped upon a bolt of lightning and charged angrily down the mount to the plains of Midgard. The first thing that Thorr noticed was the torn and tattered remains of the Venterken Tristann and his anger was fueled even further.

Thorr let out a bellow of rage at the dishonour shown to one of the chosen kings of his father Odin, calling down a massive surge of energy and a lightning bolt struck before him and cracked the land. Both armies had paused in their fighting to witness the coming of Thorr and the terrible rage he rained down upon the land. Each army had backed away from the other, While the crack in the earth spread until it had separated them. Widening, it spread until there was a mighty gap and water from the northern and southern oceans quickly flooding into fill it creating a giant channel between. Separating old Val'hal and the Aesir lands of the Cweord, The planes of Midgard had been sundered.

Raising a stone from beneath the waters of the channel, Thorr claimed it as a place of neutrality. There he called forth the leader of the two armies, Bjorn Tristansson and Vulkengarr Morfansson. Both leaders boarding a ship met on the giant island. When they stood before the mighty goethir of thunder, Thorr chastised them both for their actions. He forbade either from spilling the other's blood for ever. Forbade the two people from mating with one another and named the island truce-stone and forced both to agree that in the future if either had a grievance with the others whether the leaders themselves or their peoples, They would meet on Truce stone to try and find a solution. Placing his hammer Mjolnir on a giant rock at the center of the island, he swore them to an oath of peace. He told them that none but him could ever remove the hammer as long as both people remained peaceful toward one another. But he warned them, whichever violated the truce made there, Thorr would lift Mjolnir from its perch and wield it against the offending party. Then Thorr asked them how it all came about that they were fighting. When they explained the story, naming Luk'khen as the goethir who had instigated them to war and had shown each their racial differences to the other, Thorr raged once more, vowing to seek out his adoptive brother. From then on the people were to know Luk'khen as Loki the trickster and to never again treat with him. Then, bidding the leaders farewell and peace, Thorr left in search of his brother and the other goethir that Loki claimed were being held captive. But that is another story....

Dwarven Drinking Song

- from the Stoneaxe Region

Take the cask, pass it 'round
listen to that sloshin sound!
of Stout!

Tap the boot, slam the fist
Tell 'em to bring more o' this
….ale!

Sit th' girls upon me lap
pour 'er more from the tap
Some rum!

The tavern 'as been full today
you know what I'm 'bout ta say!
Stout!

What's better than some Gold
Listen how this storee's told
Some wine!
[Wot?! Wine? Who said that?]
    [Uh… Ale?]
Aye! Ale!

Ain't seen better time then these
not when I been on the sea's
Wit rum!

Fill the cups, roll the bones
One more 'fore sendin home
Some Rum!

Dwarven smiths strikes the steel
bowin' front o' kegs they kneel
    [Filled wit wot gents?]
Ale!

Ain't been home not seen the wife
an for it I've a better life
with Stout!

Demons, orcs and goblins be
damned
Wouldn't last against me mam
And Ale!

Awright, awright, its time to end
but how's it that we be sent?
Wit Rum!

But one more shot, jus' one
more keg
Saved wit' in me wooden leg
Ale!

THE ROAD OF THE SEVEN SISTERS BOOK II:

MAGE FIRE

Cerridwen pointed to each of the cards, at the point where the road lay. "All of you, your sisters, even your orc friend and the raven haired gentleman here." She pointed to Kayden. "You walk along this road. It is a hard road, but its truth is in the pain that will come with it. Each section of the road will represent its own trials, tests that you must each pass."

"And these cards?" Asked Marlaya, pointing to the two cards in the center of the 'V' formation, which still sat-face down.

"The top one," began Cerridwen, explaining. "Is your potential. And the other below it is your aspirations, what you wish to achieve in your deepest heart, your strongest desire. But only by surviving the other seven cards, discovering the meaning of this last one," She pointed now at 'Marlaya's card. "Will you live to see these two cards come to pass."

"May I see them?"

The woman looked at her for a long time, neither amused nor ridiculing, only curiosity in her expression, one green eye slightly more squinted than the other, as if asking Marlaya if she were sure.

"If I show them to you," she spoke finally, "there will be no turning back from your course. You will have decided the Fate of not only yourself, but that of your sisters as well. So I ask you, is this a risk you are willing to take?"

Marlaya stared back at the woman for a very long time. This time it was not curiosity in the woman's eyes, but a stone-cold seriousness. Marlaya thought it over. What would Sabine do? She wondered. Sabine was fearless. But would she be in the presence of this woman, *Cerridwen*, the wild cauldron goddess, a daemon of the Gods. Or would Sabine feel fear for the first time?

"Show me," she said finally.

"*This is my potential,*" she said to herself. "*And now my aspiration,*" She added as the next card was turned.

Her breath caught in her throat and her eyes misted as she felt an overwhelming swell of emotion balled up in her chest. The scene behind the woman on 'her' card in the formation, that which showed a couple with children, had been blown up to a large size and made up the entirety of this card. A woman that looked again like Marlaya knelt next to a man whose back was facing those who looked on. The woman held a book in her hands and was clearly reading to two of the children, while five others ran, stood or lay in various positions nearby. One of them looked to be attempting to catch a butterfly in a net. Above them, in the sky, though it was a visibly sunny day, seven stars blazed brightly.

"W-What does this mean?" She stammered.

"Whatever you want it to, Marlaya." The woman answered. "Whatever you want it to."

MYFLOR'S NIGHTLY DEVOTIONALS

As recorded by Michael Ravenheart

Thirteen, The Covenant of Aradia is, Queen of Light, Princess of magick, Daughter of the Sun and Moon, dispeller of the Dark.

Twelve, The Olympic Gods, Rulers of the Universe, Zeus the King and the Thunderous Spark

Eleven, Hera, the Queen of Heaven, our Lady Protectress of Brides and of mothers it is said.

Ten, Poseidon, Brother to Zeus and Father of the Seas; Earthshaker and Tidal Wave, the Hoppocampuses led.

Nine, Hades of the Nine Gates of Tartaros; Hospitable One, Brother to Zeus and Ruler of the Underworld, land of the Dead

Eight, Power-seeking Ares God of blood lust and war; Destroyer and seducer; Supreme Warrior

Seven, is the Speedy Hermes, Argus Slayer, Mercurial One; Messenger, Philosopher and Divine Healer

Six, Bold Athena, battle stategist and the Weight of Justice; Grey-eyed One full of Wisdom and Zeus's favored

Five, Hephaestos, master Smith of the Gods; deformed, yet wise. Aphrodite's husband, maker of the Archblade

Four,   is the Goddess Hestia of the Hearth; warmth of the Home, 4-Corners she dwells; fires are lit and burning Red.

Three,   Artemis of the Triple moon; Huntress of the Silver Bow; Goddess of the Wild hunt and Protectress o'er childbed

Two,   The Sensual Aphrodite, representing Love and the Known of Souls; Sexual expression, fire of the loins, desires fed.

One,   The Great Apollo, Sun God of Prophecy; husband of Artemis and Father of Aradia; God of Architecture, Music & Healing.

"These are my Gods. They and I are equal and One, and I and They are many. Bless me this Night and thank you for all that I was allowed to accomplish this day, and for the gifts bestowed upon me."

-Myrflor Woodvalley-

ELVISH HYMN

Orosta Avalonn' en Dharasha
Caitala Otani Itan
Arayante Lu'umenguenta'ah
Caitale ek Malon Otani
Ataran yuleh hruvalye Namarie
Caitale Avatea,

An Elvish Hymn of Prophecy

Translation:

Ascension of Shining Truth's Destiny
your people reign
(In the) chronicle of the Daybringer
you are the rising light of your people
to save them, look to the veil
(to) your.... Becoming.

Wood Nymph – doodle by Keith Morrissette

SERENITY GLOSSARY

A'lonna- Elven word for circle. Also, a popular Elven name, esp. among the noble classes.

Aldari- The name of the sub-race of Elves considered the High-Born. Racial mix of Elves consisting of Alnari and Angelic blood.

Alnari- Core race of Elves, considered the 'Low-born.' Historically, this race are the originators of all Elven lines. It is said that this race of Elves descended from the tribal peoples of Ayerlore (Avalon).

Ayerlore- Also called, 'Avalone,' this large Island country exists in the far western ocean and is surrounded by a volatile ring of active volcanoes, shrouded in thick mists; and is guarded by a giant sea monster called Charybdis. Home of the original line of Alnari and is the namesake of the Royal Isle of New Avalon in Ry'gel.

Aradia- Royal Goddess of Magick and Ritual. She is the Divine Dottir of the Gods Apollo and Artemis. She is the twin of the Triple Goddess, Morrighan, whose mother is the Titan Goddess Hekate. Aradia is the Guardian of the Magickal Well of Pneumos.

Ata- Father, dad, daddy in the Elven dialect.

Avatea- Elven word meaning, "to become."

Bannerhouse- These 'minor houses' are families who have pledged or owe their allegiances to one of the thirteen "Ruling Houses," in the Elven Kingdom of Ry'gel.

<u>Bloodmetal</u>- Believed to be the divine blood of the Titan Kronos. It is actually a molten or hard metal coming from lava flows in the mountains all over Proxima, with the largest concentrations in Ry'gel. It is the lightest, yet hardest metal in existence, and has some of the highest levels of pneumos known to Dwarves and Elves. The Dwarves forge magickal weapons and armour for themselves and for their allies, the Elves. Only a trained Dragonsmith can forge items from this special metal.

<u>Bloodryder</u>- These are dragonriders, the most elite cavalry until in the Elven military. Membership in the Bloodryder Corps is by invitation only, and reserved, until recently, for the Aldari class of Elves exclusively.

<u>Bloodsong</u>- This is the resonating, pneumonic "song," or ring that exists inside of bloodmetal. Only a Dragonsmith can hear its "song".

<u>Calusari/Mage</u>- Senior members of the Temple of Aradia, also called the "White Robes." These are Mages, Masters of Magick and often, they serve as teachers in the Mage Akademie.

<u>Chrono</u>- Measure of time consisting of one hour.

<u>Constable</u>- Civil protectors, like police. Some branches consist of confessors, who magickally force confessions from criminals. These men and women can only come from either House Ravencrest or one of its "banners."

<u>Croteauan Guard/Priests</u>- Consisting of members of bannerhouse, Croteau in the Royal lands of Laertes. Their house is responsible for the care of, and management of the realm's burial sites and as Priest/esses of

Macaria, they perform the burial rites. They are also the tally-keepers of the dead on a battlefield and are responsible for informing the families of the fallen.

Dignitas- Earned, "Honour" program overseen by the Office of Dignitas Registry. This program measures a man or woman's reputation and by building one's dignitas, can serve to open doors into higher careers and social status that may otherwise be unavailable to some of the lower classes of Elves. In this way, any Elven man or woman, no matter in what class they were born, can rise in the ranks of their country.

Dragonknight- Knight-soldier in Ry'gel's most elite military Order.

Dragonsmith- An individual (usually Dwarven), who can "hear" the "bloodsong," inside of bloodmetal, determining what type of Magick it can harness, therefore determining what the "smith" will ultimately forge from the metal. These individuals are entrusted with the secrets to its very unique forging process. There has only been one person in all of Ry'gel's history who was not a Dwarf, who has "heard the bloodsong." This was an Elven man named Raylor Smallfort, who was taught by the Dragonsmith, Gordek Mountainborn.

Lady/Lord-knight- A Knight of noble birth and/or an individual who has served nobly in the Order of Dragon Knights.

Lira- Elven word meaning mother, mom, mommy.

Mantika- Means of divination used by a "Mantikus," or seer. Can be either cards, stones, sticks, or scrying balls, or pools.

<u>Naglari</u>- Race of elves whose lineage comes from the mixing of the Alnari and the humans. Because humans are considered to be one of the worst races in Proxima, and are often discriminated against by Elven classes, to mate with one is considered in bad taste, and looked down upon, earning these elves the moniker, "Dark Elves." Only the pairing of a human and an Alnari would result in the creation of a "dark elf." Mating a human with an Aldari would cancel out any human trait, as an Aldari's blood is stronger, and therefore a Dark Elf would not be created. But what Nobel Aldari in their right mind would mate with a human?

<u>Nosta</u>- Elven word mean, "Birthday."

<u>Orucani/Orc</u>- A sub-race of an ancient people known as the Orugatai, who were believed to be master builders and engineers, before the coming of the "Doom," and long before the Elves ever set forth on Ry'gel. The orcs are related to the race of Dwarves…but don't ever let a dwarf hear you saying that!

<u>Palladium</u>- One of thirteen bloodcrystals imbued with powerful magickal energy that can weaken and painfully torture a demon. These are very rare gems, and the Palladium are fashioned into symbols of either Gods, or the House that they reside in. The Palladium were given into the safe keeping of the 13 Ruling Houses in order to spread them throughout the realm, that creates a barrier keeping demons from being able to enter the country.

<u>Ruling Houses</u>- These are the Thirteen Houses that rule Ry'gel. They are houses Ravencrest, Laertes, Valkyrie, Eversoar, Gryffyn, Avarin, Thurber, Juno, Keto, Arachne/Achidnae, Draclunari, Annwin, and Silvermane.

<u>Pneumos</u>- This is the well of power that resides in all of Creation. When manifested, harnessed, and used, it is better known as Magick.

<u>Squire</u>- Young man or woman who is taken at the ages of between 13 and 20, to become aid and apprentice to a liege-knight. These individuals will serve around seven years before being oathed (knighted) by the Archangel at Arkfall, receiving a long sword as a gift from their liege-knight, using part of the funds from their "squiring dowry."

<u>Swords-N-Sceptres</u>- A role-playing game played mainly amongst the wealthier citizens of Ry'gel. The game has become popular even within the lower classes. Originally created as a strategy game for generals in the military, it has grown to popularity even traveling all the way here to Earth.

<u>Seven Sisters</u>, The- Legendary story in Ry'gel detailing the lives of seven heroic women in the country's history. These seven women hailed from the Amazonian Isle of Themis-kyra, and became famous during the "Usurper wars," a particularly dark time in Ry'gel's history before meeting their untimely end by the overwhelming forces of the usurper-queen Meghan Ultor. Also, the name of the Bardic Poem written about them.

<u>Vlandyr</u>- Elvenoid hybrid of vampiric creatures who inhabit the southern lands of Ry'locke called Lamia. These creatures can live on meat for physical sustenance and crave both blood and pneumos as the source of their strength and longevity.

<u>Valkyrie</u>- Elven word meaning "Lady of Valour/Honour." Also, the name of one of the most prolific Elven Ruling Houses in Ry'gel beside the Ravencrests. This house of warrior-women boasts a very matriarchal system in which most noble women refuse to marry or stay married to any man who rises in rank above them.

About the Author

Lord Michael Ravenheart is a professed Hellenic, following the sacred pathways of the Olympic Gods and Goddesses. He has been studying ancient cultures, languages, myths, prophecies and people all of his life. He has been writing for almost as long and has finally decided to put to the written and narrated word, his account from the history of the planet Proxima and its elven 'aldari and alnari' citizens. He has lived the life of a warrior, recluse, a rogue, rancher and the resident in a penal colony and now he wishes to settle into the calm and serene life of war, dragons, elves and faeries, orcs, politics and love, daemons, angels, and high adventure on his island home in Greece. Join him for a spot of tea, some Avarin wine, or even some Valkyrie mead. He would be happy to share a tale or two with you travelers and perhaps you might walk away better for it. To learn more about Lord Michael Ravenheart visit his facebook Michael Ravenheart @ Facebook the Facebook/Groups @ The Road of the Seven Sisters, or visit his website at: www.michaelravenheartauthor.com

www.ingramcontent.com/pod-product-compliance
Lightning Source LLC
Chambersburg PA
CBHW060555100726
47907CB00005B/1366